Auctioned to The Pack

Howl's Edge Island: Omega For The Pack (Book 2)

Layla Sparks

D1710596

Contents

Things to Know...

Omegaverse Terms

A few things to know regarding the omegaverse world. The people in the omegaverse display a more canine or wolflike behavior. Some books involve shifting into wolves. This series will have minimal shifting.

Here are some terms that will be helpful to know (*note: these definitions pertain to my stories and not all omegaverse stories):

Omega: A female or male who would often have multiple partners to help them during heats. Usually has a particular scent that alphas find very appealing and unable to resist.

Beta: Like a normal human in the wolf world

Alpha: Top of the food chain, and they gravitate to omegas. They also have a scent that attracts omegas.

Delta: Ferocious and deadly

Slick: Secretion from the privates

Heat: A period where an omega needs to mate - akin to ovulating in human females.

Knot: When an alpha mates and omega, and the base of the penis swells, locking the alpha and omega in place.

Rut: Alphas can go into rut phase, similar to heat. Sometimes an omega's heat will bring it on.

Scent blockers: Can come in pills or as a cream. Blocks an omega scent from attracting alphas.

Heat Suppressants: Stops an omega from going into heat

Content Guide

If you don't have any triggers, please skip this page to avoid spoilers! For any questions regarding triggers, please email: author_laylasparks@yahoo.com

- Double Penetration

- Menage

- Group Play

- Backdoor (anal) Play

- Past non-consent (in her past)/ parental abuse

- Pregnancy

- Domestic Discipline/ Spanking

- Degradation play (very mild)

- Claiming bites

- Edging

Prologue

Keera

At sixteen, most teen girls weren't best friends with their moms. But I was.

And it was all my fault she was murdered.

"I feel like an outcast sometimes," I complained, licking my ice cream cone. My mother and I were walking down the dirt path of our garden, surrounded by a huge expanse of trees around us. Flower beds littered the garden since my mother loved planting.

"Why is that Keera?"

"I just do. I hate it."

Mom wrapped her gray cardigan tighter around her from the gust of wind.

"I know you're going to do great amazing things in life, and everyone will be jealous. Whenever you set your mind to do something, it usually happens. Your stubbornness sets you apart."

I shook my head.

"School isn't the same for an omega. I have to act a certain way and not look at alpha teachers in the eyes. It's not fair."

"Life is changing every day on Howl's Edge," Mom said. "One day, omegas will be free to act how they want and do whatever they want.

But for now, be patient and let everything sort itself out."

While she was talking, I suddenly felt the hairs on the back of my neck rise. I looked around the dense trees surrounding our open backyard.

"I think there's someone there," I whispered.

"What is it, honey?" asked my mom, unconcerned, looking around.

Then he appeared. A tall man with scraggly red hair appeared in the tree line, deliberately walking towards us. He had intent and purpose in his eyes, looking directly at me. His beady black eyes looked merciless. There was something wrong with the way he looked at me.

"Is that an alpha?" I asked. His demeanor said it all. Alphas walked with a certain gait and posture of arrogance.

"He seems to be. I wonder what he wants and what he's doing on our property," she hissed.

"Mom, we need to go. He looks creepy," I said, stopping my mom and gently tugging her elbow. It wasn't a good idea to confront him. His eyes were on my face, completely zoned in on me and getting closer. It felt like my feet were glued to the ground. My pulse raced with fear.

"Get away!" yelled my mom as she stood before me, blocking my view of the creepy red-haired man.

"I want her. The omega," he rasped, trying to get around my mom. "Get outta the way, beta *bitch*."

"I'm her mom. Stay the fuck away!" she screamed, punching his chest.

That move aroused his anger. And everything happened in a split second after that. He picked my mom up, and a scream stuck in my throat. He flung her against the concrete wall. Blood rushed down the wall, and all I could do was scream. Everything moved in slow motion around me.

My father came out of nowhere and began beating the alpha to a pulp on the ground.

"That's my wife!" he screamed at the alpha. When he looked over at Mom, his fists stopped raining down on the alpha.

The alpha took that chance to crawl away and run off into the trees, his face bloody and torn. My dad cradled my mother's head as he knelt next to her. She looked so frail. Her eyes were open, and chills went through my trembling body. He felt for her heartbeat, and then he burst into tears.

She was dead. My mother was dead.

My breathing came in shallow breaths. Harsh and fast. *What the hell just happened?*

I walked over to my dad, and he held a hand up, stopping me. He looked up at me with bloodshot eyes filled with pure rage.

"This is all your fault," he growled.

I stood there in shock. My mouth open.

And this was the day I lost both my parents.

Chapter 1

Eleven Years Later

Keera

"Congratulations on your twins," I exclaimed, handing one of the babies to Tiana, a new omega mother at *Howl's Honor Hospital*. The nurse settled the second baby over the young mother's chest. The joy on her face and all of her alphas' faces were palpable as they gazed upon the squirming bundles.

As the nurses cleaned up the afterbirth, I washed my hands and pulled out my clipboard. My heart ached as I gazed at the alphas' love and admiration for their omega who had given birth.

I wish I had an alpha pack who cared about me.

But I knew it would never happen with a father like mine. I was doomed to be alone.

Sighing, I blew a piece of my hair away from my face that escaped my hairnet as I jotted down the babies' time of birth, weight, and necessary information to register them. Every baby was registered, especially if an omega was born. Omegas were discernable with the wolf claw mark on their right shoulder, and they were rare.

As I wrote, the words on the paper blurred. My strength was sapped, and I knew I was getting tired from all the overtime I put in to avoid going home and facing my dad.

"We got it, Dr. Keera," said Jade, taking my clipboard. She was a fellow omega and one of my nurses under my charge. "You go and get some rest. You look like you're about to faint after this nightlong birth."

"Thanks, Jade," I said, grateful as I let her take the clipboard. "I think I'll grab a snack."

She nodded as she filled in the rest of the information, her eyebrows furrowed. I looked back one last time, seeing the new family huddled around the babies. I always thought I'd get used to it, but it hurt.

Every fucking time.

There was probably something wrong with me. No normal person would be upset seeing a happy family like that.

As I walked down the sterile white halls, I passed by several curtained rooms with omega females screaming or cursing while giving birth. Three females in labor were on this floor, and two overworked doctors were rushing about. They needed to hire more doctors.

I was about ready to pass out. I needed food now before going home because who knew when I would get food next. I removed my bloody scrubs, throwing them into a large bucket. Walking into the break room, I groaned upon seeing Tim, my beta coworker who was

9

obsessed with me, digging inside the fridge. I sat far away on the long table, placing my head in my hands to try and relax.

"Keera!" he said when he was finished rummaging around.

I took a few deep breaths with my head still down. Then I steeled myself as I looked up.

"Hey, Tim," I said, putting on a fake smile.

He still seemed to think we were besties even after I told him I didn't want anything else to do with him after we kissed once. And that kiss was totally out of nowhere. We were in the storage room, and I wasn't thinking straight after the holiday Christmas party at work. Ever since that day, I kept trying to avoid him, but he always got that glint in his eye, thinking we had something.

"Tough shift, huh?" Tim asked, his eyes bloodshot as he drank his iced coffee.

"Yep, for sure," I said, exhausted. He rolled a water bottle down the table, and I snatched it, downing it. "Thanks."

"Kind of stupid that we have to slave away while the other doctors are upstairs in that fancy meeting of theirs."

"What fancy meeting?" I asked, setting down my water and straightening in my chair.

"The directors of this hospital and the doctors are having a meeting with the donors," he said. "You know. Like the big wigs who donate a shit ton of money to the hospital."

"Why didn't they tell me?"

I didn't have to ask. I already knew they were biased against omegas like myself in the work field. I worked my ass off, but it wasn't enough for them, apparently.

"I have no idea," he said blithely, plopping into a chair beside me, trying to flex his spindly arms.

"You said the meeting was upstairs?"

"Yeah, but don't go if you're not invited," he warned.

"I don't give a shit," I said, my heart pounding.

I walked out of the break room and up the stairs. It wasn't fair that I wasn't invited to the meeting, and it felt like one of those instances where I'd have to stand up to myself.

I'd like to be known for my skills. I've been with this hospital for a year, and they still didn't have the decency to tell me anything. The bias against my kind wasn't something that I could get over. I never even thought I could be a doctor, but after Mom died, I was determined. When the omega scholarships were offered as a chance to progress omegas on Howl's Edge, I jumped at the chance. My father was against it initially, but I convinced him we'd have money if I did. It was the worst mistake I ever made because that ended up with my father taking every penny of all my paychecks.

I stood outside the door to the meeting room and pressed my ear to it. *Should I just go inside?* Suddenly the door opened, and I fell headfirst, crashing into someone's hard chest. He held me by my arms to stop me from falling on my face completely.

Face heated, I quickly stood up, straightening my black blazer.

The stranger I crashed into had long white hair mixed with silver, carefully trimmed at his shoulders. He had the oddest purple eyes I've ever seen. Almost electric. His face was weathered, but he looked energetic and young, wearing a plum suit with a shiny purple tie. I immediately got a whiff of his strong peppermint smell. Signifying his alpha-hood.

My body immediately responded, and a whiff of my orange scent

11

escaped the scent blocker cream I had slathered on this morning.

"Why hello there," he said, extending out his hand.

"Hi," I said, dumbstruck. He must be one of the millionaire alpha donors. He clearly looked the part. "Nice hair."

"My barber has the magic touch," he said. His voice held authority and a touch of sarcasm. He looked like he didn't take himself too seriously. "May I have *your* magic touch?"

He looked down, and I followed his gaze.

I gasped. He had an obvious erection. This guy was not shy. A definite alpha hole.

"No! *What the fu-*," I started to say.

"What is going on?" said a sharp female voice interrupting us.

"Ugh," I muttered, I despised talking to her. But this alpha was even worse. Lucia was the director of *Howl's Honor Hospital* and an alpha female. She flipped her long blond hair back, her nose in the air. My few interactions with her were short and to the point.

She wasn't exactly warm and friendly.

"I heard there was a meeting going on?" I asked innocently.

"You can get back to work. The meeting's almost over," said Lucia. *Bitch.*

"Why can't I join the meeting too?" I challenged.

"Yes, why not?" asked the stranger with the weird silver hair, butting in. I wanted to smack him but held myself back.

Lucia looked perturbed when he asked the question, scrambling for an answer. *Since he was a millionaire donor, of course.* I wanted to roll my eyes.

"We're short-staffed at the moment and they need her," she said. "May I escort you back to the meeting, Mr. Lustfur?"

"You have like every doctor in there," I said, gesturing towards the door. "I don't understand why I wasn't told, at least."

"You're an omega. Why do you care about this stuff?" she stated, her face twisted in disgust. She said it like it should make sense to me.

And to just be grateful that I was even working here.

"Whoa," said Mr. Lustfur. He looked taken aback.

"I'm interested," I said stubbornly. "I would like to join the meeting."

"You're done," said Lucia, pissed. I embarrassed her in front of someone important. "Give me your badge."

My stomach immediately sank. My dad came to mind.

He was going to kill me. *Fuck my life.*

"Fine," I huffed, removing my lanyard from around my neck and flinging my badge at Lucia. She looked shocked. My heart was pounding hard from adrenaline. "You can stuff it."

As I turned to walk out, I saw Jade standing there with her mouth open, shocked at what just happened.

I waited outside of the hospital building for my ride. My dad ensured he would pick me up and drop me off at work. It was rare for omegas to drive or to walk around freely without their guardian or alpha pack.

"Are you going to find another job?" asked Jade, standing outside with me. The mood was glum, and I dreaded my father's wrath when I would tell him I lost my job. Jade, along with everyone else, thought my life was perfect, but it was far from perfect.

"I'm going to have to find another job," I said. "I can't sit around at

13

home all day."

"Do you want to go to the Omega Ball tomorrow with me? Now that you're fired and all," she said.

"Not a good idea," I said. But, honestly, I didn't want to tell her that my father was the reason I didn't go anywhere or do anything without his express permission. He had instilled that alpha order in me ever since I was little to obey. And it was hard to fight against or rebel.

"Why? It'll be fun, and it will take your mind off stuff."

"I've never been to the Omega Ball. Isn't it dangerous? All the alphas showing up to court omegas?"

"Every year, there's strict security. Nothing is going to happen," Jade said.

The ball was only for omegas to meet alpha packs. I *wanted* to meet an alpha pack to escape my hellish life.

"How about I meet you here tomorrow at eight am?"

Maybe my dad could drop me off thinking I was going to work. I couldn't be in the house tomorrow, because I didn't want him to know about my job loss yet.

"Why that early? You're not even working tomorrow," laughed Jade.

"I can't tell my dad that I lost my job," I said. Her eyes widened. Jade and I were good work friends, but I wasn't sure how much to trust her. "So I have to pretend I'm working."

"I get it," she said softly, looking down. It looked like she regretted giving me a hard time earlier. "I'll bring you back here around your usual time that you get off from work."

"Okay, that works then," I smiled. Inside, I felt a little giddy at doing this. I was going to the *Omega Ball*. My stomach was knotted

14

in nervousness and excitement. My dad pulled up in his beat-up small green car, and all the butterflies in my belly disappeared.

"Bye, Keera," waved Jade.

"See ya," I said as I walked towards the car.

I swung open the passenger-side door and sat inside to the scowl of my father. He had a short stature and a permanent resting bitch face ever since Mom died.

"Close the door, hurry up," he snapped. "So slow!"

I shut the door, and he pinched my thigh when I finally did. *Ass.*

Chapter 2

Jatix

I sat through the rest of the torturous donor meeting, bored out of my mind.

The beautiful omega who crashed into me was still ingrained in my mind. She was a stunner, and she didn't know it. I loved it when a female didn't know her allure. My hard-on was apparent, and I didn't give a shit who saw it.

After the meeting was over, I rushed into the men's stall. I quickly unzipped my pants and imagined her as I stroked myself. Her narrow eyes and pink lips invaded my mind. My breathing quickened as I wrapped my hand tighter around my ever-growing cock. I imagined her laying under me, legs spread open, her face flush and sweating.

The little doctor calling out my name over and over as I slapped her ass...My cock deep inside her until she couldn't bear it.

Fuck.

I came with a growl, collapsing against the door of the stall, my breath coming out in gasps.

It had been a long time since I saw an omega.

Ever since my pack lost to the Frostcrown Pack, the females stayed away. I was annoyed my reputation was messed up now, but I was going to fix it. Grant and his pack were going to regret what they did. We had made a deal that they would hand over an omega, and even though Tiana stayed for less than an hour, I was angry she was taken away.

But after seeing this omega doctor today, my anger lessened. Her witty remarks and sharp humor were entertaining.

And I wanted more of it.

After cleaning myself up, I walked around the hospital, looking for the omega doctor. I needed to talk to her again. She was unmated without the smell of an alpha on her. I knew she was an omega even though she tried to hide it behind her scent blockers. As an experienced older alpha, I could smell past the scent blockers. Her scent was of summer oranges in the sun, and I couldn't get enough.

"Can I help you with something?" asked a skinny male with minimal hair. He looked like a newborn rat, and his badge said *Tim*.

"I'm looking for the omega doctor," I said.

"Oh, you mean Keera? She left already," he replied.

Keera, huh? Beautiful name.

I wasn't happy about her getting fired. Not at all. The hospital wasn't going to get a penny until they reinstated Keera but I had to talk to her first.

"Alright, thanks," I said gruffly, walking towards the exit.

As I drove away from the hospital, I couldn't stop thinking about her.

I might never be able to find her, especially since she was fired. I had no idea where this girl lived. Maybe I'd have Darius, my pack's bodyguard, look for her. Darius was the only Delta in my pack and had no mercy. I turned left at the stop sign after waiting for all the damn people to cross the street. I needed to get home and tell my pack what had happened. I kept remembering her alluring dark eyes. She was a determined girl who knew what she wanted. My pack would enjoy her if I ever found her.

I parked in front of my house. Some people would call it a mansion.

After locking my car door, I took in the beautiful scenery as I always did of Howl's Edge. The palm trees and ocean lay in front of my house, where I loved to sit and contemplate. The house was passed onto me by my dead father. My alpha mother refused to live in the house because of me, and I didn't give a fuck. She could do what she wanted.

I walked inside.

"Hey, Jatix!" shouted Shawn as he washed the dishes. His twin Silus sat in the living room, flipping through channels.

"I'm back, darlings," I said sarcastically, sitting down on the dining room chair. "I want to talk to you all about something. Where the fuck is Darius?"

"He's probably out smashing wood or something," muttered Silus, setting down the remote with his heavily tattooed arm. "What do you want, J?"

"I'm here," said Darius, walking in from the back door.

"Gather 'round men," I announced. Silus looked annoyed, Darius's facial expression never changed, and Shawn's chubby face looked eager to hear the news. "I met an omega today that I'm sure I'll never see again."

"So?" said Darius, crossing his arms over the long silver chains that hung from his neck. He was a large delta with intimidating features and spiky blond hair.

"Was she beautiful?" asked Shawn dreamily, his chubby hands resting on the kitchen counter and looking at me eagerly.

His twin brother, Silus, was more laid back and couldn't care less. These men had all the beta women they could want in the past. But it had been a long time since a female stepped into this home.

"She was beautiful," I said. "But I don't think I'll ever find her. I think it's time we went to the Omega Auction and purchased ourselves an omega."

"No way," Shawn interrupted. "She would never like us. I don't want some boring omega forced to serve our sexual needs."

"I'm sure she'll end up liking you," I said, rolling my eyes. "This week, we should check out what's there and start shopping."

"It sounds hot," said Silus, flipping his mop of brown hair away from his face. "Make sure she's cute."

"No omega," said Darius, shaking his head. "It's a bad idea."

"How about you help me pick out an omega?" I offered Darius. I had no idea why he hated omegas so badly, but I really needed him onboard and excited about this decision. Darius perched on the edge of a chair, looking at the white floors, contemplating.

Finally, he sighed.

"If we really need an omega here, fine, I'll help you pick one out," said Darius. "Why not a beta?"

"I would like to commit this time," I said. "Like have a serious relationship with an omega. Have babies."

"Babies?" guffawed Silus, almost falling off the couch. I scowled. "You aren't ready for that shit."

"Shut it," I growled. "Yes, I want babies. And I want to fucking impregnate our new omega."

Chapter 3

Keera

"Where's your paycheck, you useless bitch?" asked my dad, his spittle flying in my face. I could smell the alcohol on his breath already and worried if we would get home safely.

"It doesn't come until next Friday," I said quietly.

I stayed silent as my dad ranted and raved about how useless I was and that I was such a burden. The same old stuff.

"I'm sick and tired of driving you to work," said Dad, the car weaving off the road. I nearly had a heart attack. He was never this drunk while driving. Ever since Mom died, his drinking had gotten significantly worse. And my paychecks went to his gambling addiction. I had no idea how he paid the mortgage on the house or the bills. He wasn't the same dad at all from before Mom died.

Whenever I checked my bank account, it was always negative. Getting him off my bank account was impossible since the alpha guardian had the right to an omega's money. The bank would always listen to him. I had nowhere to go without money, and leaving Howl's Edge Island was out of question. I wouldn't know anyone and would be penniless if I had managed to sneak past the tight security. Howl's Edge officers were on every corner, watching who entered and left the island.

If I stayed out in the streets, I could be prey. The Wild Wolfmen who lived on the outskirts of town always prowled for an omega. Growing up, I heard that they used omegas for sacrificial purposes but they could just be stories. Then there were alphas in the streets dealing off omegas like we were commodities.

"Why don't you let me drive the car then?" I offered.

"Omegas don't drive, stupid."

I thought about Jade and how she was able to drive. My dad's mind was still trapped in the old days, refusing to see omegas succeed, or he just personally hated me. Just a property to alphas. But he also blamed me for Mom's death.

And I believed him.

The killer had come for me when I turned sixteen, and my scent had started to emerge. If I had known, I would have never left the house and put my mom in danger. I would have taken my scent blocker pills earlier. We could have sat in the house that day playing Monopoly. Anything besides taking the dreaded walk behind our house.

There were so many things I could have done.

Later, once we were home, my hands shook as I opened the heat suppressant bottle as my dad watched. He had a grim expression as I looked at the pill in my hand.

"I can't keep taking two of these a day. One is enough, " I said. "I'll never be able to have kids."

"Well, you don't need any kids," he growled, slapping my hand. The pill dropped to the ground as my hand stung. "Pick it up and eat it."

His face was twisted in fury, and I felt my pride dwindle as I picked up the pill, which I quickly downed. My stomach growled since I hadn't eaten, but he didn't care as he dragged me by the arm to my room. I was flung inside as he locked the door from outside. The only light that streamed into the room was the moonlight shining through the window.

There was no curtain, and no furnishing, except for a single thin mattress in the middle of the room. I was never allowed blankets in case it would trigger my nesting instinct, which would then cause me to go into heat. My dad was extra careful about that for some reason. Sometimes the heat suppressant pills weren't enough to keep an omega's heat at bay.

I stood at the window watching the moon as tears pricked my eyes.

Sometimes I would remember how my dad was when I was a child. Before Mom died, he was so loving and caring. But he became a completely different person after she died. A monster I couldn't handle. I stripped off my clothing, pulling on ripped-up cotton pants with a checkered black and white shirt that didn't match. I curled up on the mattress, feeling the hard ground on my side. It was always cold in here.

I regretted not having eaten at work. Even a fruit bar would've helped. It's not that my dad didn't allow me to eat, it was mainly because I didn't want to be around him while he watched television in the living room. The less time I had to spend with him, the better.

I yawned as the exhaustion from work set in. As I closed my eyes, I thought about the Omega Ball that would be happening tomorrow and envisioned wearing a pretty gown with all the alphas looking at me. The last thing that I thought of was twirling in the arms of the stranger with the silver hair and purple suit. Mr. Lustfur was his name. He was so full of himself, but something about his assuredness turned me on like no other alpha I've met.

I finally drifted off to sleep with thoughts of dancing in his arms while he whispered sweet nothings in my ear.

The next morning, I woke up to the alarm blaring early at seven-thirty am. I quickly shut it off and rubbed my eyes. I was still exhausted as usual from sleeping on the thin mattress. My skin was freezing from the lack of blankets, and my pajamas were torn again from stretching it over my skin for coverage to make up for the lack of sheets.

The door was unlocked. Usually, it was unlocked in the mornings so I could get ready for work, and I could smell my dad's coffee wafting upstairs. He was always in a better mood in the mornings, and there was no point in bringing up the night before. I didn't want to make him mad. After showering and pulling on my blue scrubs, I packed my best outfit for the dance in my backpack. A pair of jeans and a sparkly red v-neck shirt. I knew it wasn't a dress, but that was the best I had. The lavish gowns I daydreamed the night before was only a dream and nothing else.

I hesitantly went downstairs, nonchalantly slinging my briefcase over my shoulder.

"Let's go," my dad said, setting down his cup of coffee. He looked up. "You have to get to work bright and early for that money." That was all he cared about. I never even got to enjoy my money. I didn't know how it was to save and buy something of my own.

When he dropped me off at the hospital, I waited until he drove off before I snuck around to the back of the building. I was out of breath by the time I reached the parking lot in the back- where Jade and I agreed to meet. I didn't have a phone, so I couldn't exactly call her. My dad had the latest Eclipse Phone, while I had nothing.

I saw Jade standing by her silver car with a smile. Her hands were clasped in front of her and her black hair was done in curls around her face. She wore a simple outfit of jeans and a pink t-shirt. But I knew she was going to go all out later. She wasn't one to look simple for too long.

"Ahh, I can't believe you're coming with me this time!" said Jade. "All the other omegas are so snotty at the ball. And my family wants me to go every year, but no one wants a chubby omega."

"I'm sure you'll meet the right pack who'll love your curves," I said, wanting to get out of here as fast as possible before any co-worker saw me, or worse- the manager. I quickly got into the passenger seat and turned down the loud music she had been playing in the car.

"So what are you wearing to the ball?" Jade asked eagerly, her eyes on my dingy gray briefcase. I unzipped my bag and showed her my glittering red shirt and blue jeans. "Oh no, that won't work."

"I don't really care how I look," I protested.

"Let's go shopping. Get yourself a new dress."

25

Oh, shit.

"I forgot my card," I said quickly.

"How about you can pay me back after?" she offered as she put the car into gear. She started driving towards the mall and I realized I was suddenly stuck. I couldn't let her know I was broke and I couldn't back out of going with her the ball. I was a doctor, for fuck's sake. There was no way I'd let her know the truth of it all.

"Um, sure," I said.

The only solution was that I was going to find the cheapest dress there was.

But I soon realized that none of the dresses were cheap. We were at *Moon Cloud Mall*, and it was packed on a Saturday. It seemed as if every person on Howl's Edge was here. The beta cashiers looked overwhelmed, assisting long lines of shoppers.

I was looking through the dress rack, flipping through the dresses. My heart sank more and more as I browsed, unable to find something cheap enough. The cheaper it was, the more horrible it would look which was to be expected. I was going to just call it a day, and pretend I was too sick to go to the dance.

"How about this one?" asked Jade, holding out a pretty periwinkle blue dress.

"It's loud," I said, cringing at the dress. "I want something a little more lowkey."

I stopped rifling through the dress rack when I saw it. A dress that caught my eye.

It was a black sparkling dress with spaghetti straps and a low neck-line. The waist was tight and flowed elegantly down. Running my hands down the fabric, it was made of satin and soft to the touch. Then, I looked at the dreaded price tag, $39.99. I didn't even have a dollar to my name. Scratch that, a *penny* to my name.

"Is that the one?" asked Jade, touching the dress.

"I want to try it on first," I said before giving her a definite answer. I had to absolutely love it before going into debt for it. The shopkeeper of the store led me to the fitting rooms. Removing my scrubs, I pulled the dress on carefully over my head, scared to rip it.

"Can I see it?" asked Jade.

"I need help zipping it up," I called, and Jade was waiting on the other side of the door when I opened it. She helped zip it up, and I took a long minute as I looked in the mirror. The black dress sparkled in all the right places, accentuating my waist and butt. I never felt so pretty in life and I shyly looked at the ground.

"It's stunning," said Jade. "With just the right amount of makeup and jewelry, you might snag a hunky alpha pack."

Excitement drummed in my chest as I stared into the mirror.

During the drive to the Omega Ball, Jade's older brother Jack sat in the back of the car, and I was getting tired of their bickering as I touched up my makeup in the mirror above me.

"I don't want to see any fishy business with the alphas," said Jack.

"We're doing whatever the hell we want," said Jade. I was starting to regret taking Jack with us. The rule was that an omega needed to have an alpha guardian with them, especially for an event like this. Security would never allow us in otherwise.

Jack looked similar to his sister with his big-boned structure. Jade had wide-set dark eyes, jet-black hair, and an olive skin tone. She had taken extra care in curling her hair, and her silver eyeshadow made her features pop. After shopping at Moon Cloud Mall, we had gotten ready at Jade's house. I was surprised to see how stable and lovely her family was. She had three alpha fathers who adored her omega mother. I enjoyed being there, especially when her mom helped me do my makeup. I almost burst into tears several times, thinking about my own mother.

I had such a good time that it was seven by the time we left, even though the ball started at six.

"Wow, the palace is huge," I said as Jade drove into the crowded parking space. The Omega Ball was hosted every year by the Royal Pack. I had never been to the palace. I stared wide-eyed at the giant building draped in purple and gold. It was so beautiful and majestic.

"Remember, we need to get back to the hospital by ten," I reminded Jade. Before my dad had to pick me up from there.

"Yeah, yeah. Don't worry," she said.

My heart beat faster with excitement the closer we got to the palace.

28

Chapter 4

Darius

"**M**ake sure you're checking to see if every omega arrives with their guardian," instructed the head force of security as he made his rounds to all of us at the Royal Palace. He was a delta like myself, hoping to intimidate some of the other beta security. I rolled my eyes. I couldn't care less if an omega arrived alone at the Omega Ball.

I only took on this job because of the hefty pay I'd receive. Five thousand dollars wasn't something to sneeze at.

Adjusting my uniform, I watched as each glamorous omega made their entrance into the ballroom. I was standing at the front doors, and across from me was another Delta guard. It almost made me sick watching how uppity and stuck up the omegas looked as they gazed upon their desirable alphas. Some of the omegas looked my way fearfully, especially at the large gun strapped over my shoulder.

I didn't give a fuck. I was here to do my job, collect my pay, and then go home. As I gazed at the omegas entering the ball with their guardians, one omega in particular caught my eye. She wore a glittering black dress that hugged her stunning body but the thing that stood out to me was her downcast gaze. She looked shy and almost uncertain of herself, unable to look at anyone. As she crossed the gates, her heels snagged on the ground and she tripped.

By the time I rushed over to her, she was sitting on her butt on the ground. I helped her back on her feet, her skin soft and smooth at the touch. When she stood back up, my breath stopped. She had long black hair that shone under the palace lights with a necklace of red and silver jewels draped around her neck.

"Are you okay?" I asked, still holding her hand in mine. She grasped it, clumsily almost falling again. With her hand in mine, I felt something inside of me shift. Light entering my dark soul. Or it could be her deadly omega magic.

"Yes, sorry, I hate heels," she laughed awkwardly, trying to deflect the attention from herself. Our gaze met, and her face looked flushed and embarrassed as the guests looked at her. I didn't want to look away from those hazel eyes of hers. I detected a light scent of mandarine, or was it orange? It was emanating from her in the light breeze outside, and it was intoxicating.

She didn't want attention. *That never happened with omegas.*

"Have fun inside," I said, annoyed at myself for feeling affected by her. I walked back to my post, watching as she and her friend entered the palace. My head was spinning as I watched each omega and alpha walk inside. My job was also to ensure an alpha didn't cross boundaries with an omega. I turned my gaze to the omega with the raven-colored hair who had fallen. Thirsty alphas already surrounded her as she made her grand entrance without looking at any of them. Something about her appealed to me, but I had better get my act together.

Because she was bound to be with an alpha pack, not a guard like myself.

Chapter 5

Keera

*W**ell, that was mortifying.*

My face still burned with embarrassment as I conversed politely with the alphas who approached Jade and I, with her brother Jack hovering just behind us. I couldn't believe I tripped in front of everyone. Luckily it was just at the entrance, so it wasn't like hordes of alphas saw what happened. But the guard who approached me had seen me fall.

I could barely look him in the eyes. His large muscular stature of a Delta was intimidating and rough. But that made my heart pound like nothing else. He had spiky rust-colored hair and tattoos on his massive arms. When he held my hand, my body grew warmer. I suddenly realized I needed a mate in my life. I felt like I was falling for every male I met now. There weren't many Deltas on Howl's Edge, and to see a few here guarding the palace was crazy. I never even met one, let alone spoke to one of them. They all had guns and thick bulletproof vests. There were beta security officers in every corner, watching everyone as well.

Upon entering the palace, I was awestruck by the architecture and design. A massive dance floor made of crystal sparkled under the chandeliers. There was an elevated section of the floor where there were six thrones. Four of the biggest thrones sat the Royal Alphas. Alpha Saku was the current king of Howl's Edge. I learned all about the Royal Pack back in school. The omega Princess Lyra sat in the middle with her omega mother, Queen Ophelia. Princess Lyra was the only child that the Royal Pack had borne. Queen Ophelia had a miscarriage after Princess Lyra was born and hasn't had another child since. It was rumored that the Queen's alphas were getting restless and slept with other omegas in secret to produce an heir.

It felt like history gazing up at the Royal Pack, who were watching the ball they hosted.

"Princess Lyra looks annoyed, huh?" commented Jade, drinking lemonade that an alpha had bought for her. For some reason, Princess Lyra didn't look too happy as she gazed at the guests. She had honey blond hair, with a small silver tiara on top. She wore a light pink dress with many layers. She was scowling and constantly whispered to her mother next to her.

"She probably doesn't have many friends. Being a princess and all," I said. "Probably lonely."

Like myself.

"Hello, miss, may I have this dance?" asked an alpha wearing a nicely-pressed black suit. He had thin eyebrows and firm features.

"Sure," I said, allowing him to take my hand as he led me to the dance floor. I looked back at Jade, who winked at me as another alpha with a large frame approached her. The music was slow, perfect for dancing couples and packs. There were omegas taking turns dancing with packs of alphas, each alpha vying for the omega's attention. There were even betas and a couple of deltas also dancing with omegas. The omegas were discernable with the mark of the wolf claw on their shoulder. Some had it covered with makeup, and some showed it off proudly.

"What's your name?" the alpha asked. I awkwardly tried not to trip on my dress as he spun me. I was no expert at dancing at all.

"Keera. What's yours?" I asked.

"Voss," he replied, his gaze scanning my body. He wasn't discreet about it either, and I was starting to feel uncomfortable despite the slight wetness drenching my panties. The room was full of alpha scents all around, overwhelming my senses and sending my hormones into overdrive. I don't even think the two heat suppressants and scent blocker cream that my father made me take were enough to cover my scent.

"I need to get some air," I said, extricating myself from his grasp. His eyes flashed for a second. Then his look of annoyance was smoothed over with a large smile.

"Of course. Take your time. I'll be waiting eagerly for you," Voss said. Even his name gave me the shivers, and I didn't have a good feeling about him. I walked to the double back doors, squeezing between the people and trying not to bump into them. The omegas were perfuming like crazy and thirsty for their alpha packs. It seemed like there were fifty omegas in this palace. The alphas looked even more desperate and

34

predatory as they scanned the room for their perfect mate.

When I finally stepped foot into the beautiful gardens in the back, I took in a deep breath. The crisp air outside felt refreshing, clearing out the heady alpha scent playing havoc on my brain, making me want to pounce on an alpha's dick. The undertone of sexual tension in the ball was apparent. Walking around the garden, I felt calmer. There were only three omegas out here and an alpha flirting with them. I disliked crowded rooms, especially when they were full of alphas. It was sexy, but it was way too much stimulation for me.

As I walked, I was lost in thought. The gardens had rose bushes and different types of flowers in bunches growing everywhere. It reminded me of Mom and her garden. Ever since she died, the flowers died with her. The pathways were made of stone, and the further I walked away from the palace, the more I could hear the crickets chirping and the sound of the music fading away.

Suddenly, I heard a crackle of branches to my left. The peach trees lining the pathway blocked my view. A slew of fearful hiccups came over me, and I tried to keep my hiccups down as I craned my neck to see who was approaching. *Damn hiccups.*

A man was standing just behind the tree, watching me. I could only see his side profile but recognized his stringy red hair. I could recognize him anywhere, even from a mile away. It was my mother's killer and it felt like history was repeating itself.

I stood frozen on the stone pathway in a stupor, my heart racing out of my chest. I looked again, and he was gone. *Did I imagine things?* I quickly forced my feet to move, and I burst into the ballroom, every limb in my body shaking.

Where was Jade? *We had to go now!*

"You look like you've seen a ghost," said a male voice to my right as soon as I entered the ballroom. The sarcastic voice was familiar. I turned and saw the alpha with the long silver hair I had met at work—Mr.Lustfur.

One of the rich donors.

I took a few deep breaths. *Just calm down, Keera.*

"I think I might have," I said, my heart still pumping hard. "Your white hair is pretty ghostly."

"Haha, this omega got jokes, huh?" he said, walking closer to me. "How about I get you a drink?"

"I have to get going, Mr. Lustfur. Thank you for offering," I said, thinking about the evil I just saw outside. He could come in here anytime.

"Call me Jatix, Miss Keera," he said, his voice honey smooth as he gazed at me with those electric purple eyes. Ensnaring me and distracting me from the threat waiting just outside these doors. "May I have just one dance before you run away from me tonight?"

The memory of what I just saw began to fade as I looked into Jatix's eyes. He looked carefree and fun. Maybe what I just saw was my imagination. The killer was, after all, nowhere to be found here in the ballroom.

"You tried to show me your erect penis," I said. "That's disgusting."

"I was out of bounds," he said, looking down sorrowfully. "It was just a joke. I'm really sorry about that."

"It was a stupid joke."

"I know, and it won't happen again," he said. "Will you give me another chance? I don't want a gross alpha taking you home tonight."

My face cracked into a smile.

"Fine, but the only gross alpha here is you. I have to let you know that I'm a horrible dancer," I said, trying to see if that would deter him.

"Me too. Let's be horrible together," he said, taking my hands. He rolled with the punches and didn't take himself too seriously as we conversed about random stuff, and he talked so much shit about the alphas in the room while we danced, making me laugh every minute. He was good at making me forget about the harsh, cruel world, even for a second.

"Are you the only perfect alpha here, then?" I asked mockingly, letting him lead the dance. His hand was on the small of my back. He pulled me in closer, and we were within kissing distance from each other. My body warmed from the close contact. I couldn't help but stare at his lips, which curled into a small smile.

"Maybe I am," he answered. "I mean, look at my suit. Best dressed, I'd say."

Jatix wore an extravagant red suit lined in black with a blush-colored rose pinned to his right shoulder.

"It's nice," I said casually, knowing that would annoy him.

"It's not just *nice*," he retorted. "It's sexy and wild."

"Okay," I laughed, already forgetting about my encounter in the gardens. This alpha was a little nuts, but he was fun.

"Is your guardian here? I'd like to talk to him and ask for your hand," he said in a serious voice.

"Nope, but my friend's older brother is here," I said. He couldn't be serious, and if he was, I wouldn't mate with him. He was too risky and I was scared of falling in love.

"How about your father? What's his name?"

I suddenly remembered that I hadn't looked at the time for a while.

Looking up at the large clock on the wall, I gasped. It was freaking ten thirty. My dad was probably at my workplace now to pick me up. I prayed that he was late and drinking.

"I have to go," I said quickly, pulling away from his arms.

"Hey, what's wrong?" he asked, not releasing my forearm.

"I have to go," I said, my heart at my throat. I was terrified of what my father would do if he ever found out I mingled with a bunch of alphas. "I'm sorry, Jatix."

"When would I get to see you again?"

"Not for a long time," I said in a rush. "I have to go. It was nice getting to know you."

During the car ride to the hospital, I was biting my nails from anxiety. There was no way I would make it in time before my dad showed up at the hospital to pick me up.

"We're so late," I said. Jade tried to drive as fast as possible, but we were still late. I had changed back into my scrubs in the car and tried to remove as much makeup as possible.

"I'm sure your dad won't care waiting for a little bit," Jade tried to comfort me. "Jack, why don't you ever wear your seatbelt?"

"Aw, you're scared I might die," said Jack. "Just don't be a terrible driver, and I'll survive."

"It's important I get there as soon as possible," I stressed. I didn't want to explain that my dad was a psycho, especially when he drank at night. That his temper was unpredictable, and his rages were terrifying. There was no way she could understand. Her family was so peaceful and loving.

"Where do I park?" asked Jade when we got to the hospital. I couldn't see my dad's car anywhere, and I breathed a sigh of relief.

"Go around the back, to the parking lot, and I'll walk to the front," I said.

But when Jade drove into the parking lot in the back, my heart dropped.

My dad's car was parked, and he was standing outside of it, waiting for me with a scowl on his face.

"*Fuck*," I muttered.

Chapter 6

Jatix

D^{*amn.*}

*D*amn.
  I found the only omega I liked, and she had to run off like that. Maybe she *was* scared of my pack like all the other females. I nursed a drink in my hand, still at the Omega Ball and looking around at potential omega mates. I couldn't bring myself to talk to any of them. They were either too ditzy or hyper-eager to talk to alphas. I didn't want an omega running off to another pack when she went into heat. I was looking for a serious commitment this time.

Keera was beautiful, smart and laughed at my jokes. Omegas were normally put off by me for some reason. But not Keera.

I had to go after her.

I handed a server my empty glass and weaved my way through the crowd, looking for the runaway omega. Keera couldn't have gone too far. It had only been five minutes.

"Jatix!" called a voice. I recognized the Alpha king's voice. Groaning inside, I stopped immediately and turned. I noticed that King Saku had gotten older. His hair was white, and his body had shrunken down. Prominent wrinkles graced his face and neck.

"King Saku," I said, turning to him and bowing my head.

"How have you been, my son?" he asked, his voice frail.

"I've been excellent," I said. "And yourself?"

"I could be much better," he said. "How are you faring with your father's death?"

My father was a good friend of King Saku, carrying out dubious tasks that made my pack the most feared in Howl's Edge. My father hunted Wild Wolfmen for years, keeping the island safe. The rumors of me killing anyone who crossed me weren't true, but it was fun to entertain those stories and see the respect in the people's eyes.

"It's been five years. I've been coping," I said. In the beginning, I couldn't even get out of bed because of the grief. But as time went by, things got easier to cope with. Of course, the pain was still there. I loved my father. He was a powerful man with a big presence. During one of his raids on the wild wolfmen, a silver spear struck his heart.

"I'm afraid my time is coming soon," said King Saku. "My body has been afflicted with sickness. Only the family knows."

"Are you serious?" I asked, surprised. He was like an uncle to me. I couldn't remember the countless times my father brought me to the palace as he took care of business on the island's outskirts.

"I am," said King Saku, looking up at his family. "That's why I have a proposition to make."

"Okay?" I asked, not sure where the hell this conversation was going. If he wanted me to kill Wild Wolfmen, I wasn't interested. They were an abomination and refused to live in civilized society, only interested in taking our omegas by force.

"I would like for you to marry my daughter, Princess Lyra," he said slowly. "A strong pack like yours will make a great match to the Royal Pack. How about it?"

I looked up at Princess Lyra, who was scoffing at some of the alphas trying to talk to her. She flipped her golden hair, looking unhappy.

Oof, not my type.

"I want to thank you for the gracious offer," I said. "But King..."

"Before you refuse. I'd like you to think about it, Jatix," interrupted King Saku. "If you haven't found any prospects for your pack, consider my daughter. I know she would be in good hands."

I sighed.

"Yes, of course, I'll think about it. It would be an honor," I said, and King Saku smiled, showing his bright white dentures. If only he knew the *real* me, he would never have offered his daughter. After our conversation, I walked away, continuing my search for Keera. Finally, I walked to the front doors and pulled Darius to the side.

"She's gone, Jatix," said Darius before I could open my mouth.

"How do you know who I'm talking about?"

"She was the only omega you danced with tonight," said Darius with a smirk. The scar above his right cheek was prominent under the light.

"Did you get a license plate? Anything?"

"I can't move from my station. Plus, you're going to scare her off with your crazy sex toys and dungeon," said Darius.

"Useless ass delta," I muttered, running out of the front doors to look for her myself. She could still be out there in the parking area. I walked down each parking lot row, not seeing her pretty face anywhere. Maybe Darius was right. She might get scared of the dungeon.

I was aimlessly walking around the parking lot now.

But at the same time, I could see a part of her that wanted wild adventures. She was the type who would be open to all the crazy shit I was into. I wanted to see her spread out on the sex swing, her naked breasts jiggling and eagerly waiting to be sucked. My dick started to harden in my pants.

I needed to stop now before I had a one-night stand with a random omega.

Maybe it *was* time to look for an omega at the auction. And at least open myself up to other possibilities, regardless of what the pack thought.

Chapter 7

Keera

My heart was in my throat as I slowly stepped out of Jade's car. My dad looked furious as he stomped over to me, his orange mustache ruffling in the wind. To me, it was the most horrifying sight.

It was pathetic that I was scared of my own father. The only person in the world I didn't dare stand up to. He gripped my hair, my scalp burning as he pulled me towards the hideous green car. He did it right in front of Jade and her brother. It was the most humiliating thing to ever happen to me.

"Let her go!" shouted Jack as he got out of the car. My dad dragged me towards the passenger side.

"Where the hell were you?" he rasped in my face.

"Nowhere!" I screamed.

That set him off. He shoved me into the car headfirst. I quickly righted myself as he slammed the door with all his might- shaking the car to hell. I shut my eyes tight, trying to transport myself elsewhere in my mind. To escape the reality of the nightmare I had to live with every day.

I couldn't look at Jade's car. I didn't want to see looks of pity or shock on her and her brother's faces.

My dad jumped into the car and aggressively turned the engine on. He looked crazy-eyed as he backed the car out. He didn't even talk to me, and that's when I knew things were going to get ugly. My hands shook as I crossed my arms over my briefcase that contained my new dress.

My night of fun was completely ruined. I didn't dare look over at him for fear of setting him off. But, for some reason, his silence felt a lot worse. A lot more foreboding. *What was he planning?* When we entered the house, I wondered if I managed to somehow get out of a screaming lecture. Unfortunately, he quickly proved to me that I hadn't.

He grabbed my arm and flung me on the couch. I cried out as he twisted my arm and then let go. He sat on the couch across from me.

"Why didn't you tell me you got fired?"

How did he know that? Shit, shit, shit.

"They don't like omegas," I said, my head down. "It's not my fault."

"Since you're pretty much useless now. I have an idea," he said, scratching his mustache ominously. I could barely breathe. Whatever idea he came up with, I never had a say in it. Without money and nowhere to go, I was under his mercy.

"What is it?"

"I'm going to put you up for auction," he said gleefully, rubbing his hands together. "Our house is in foreclosure, so it's time for the big money. And I owe someone money."

It's in foreclosure because of your gambling addiction…

"I can get another job," I said quickly. I didn't want to be sold into some seedy auction, sold a group of horny alphas. It was the lowest thing to happen to an omega. It was only for the leftover omegas who couldn't find a pack.

"It's decided," he said. "Go to your room."

Biting my lip, I passed the bare living room and went into my room. The living room didn't have much because he sold as many things as possible to fund his gambling addiction. We only had a couch and a TV. Not even a rug.

It took no time for him to lock my door from the outside. I leaned against the wall, my eyes tearing up. Sliding down the wall, I sat with my knees pulled up to my chest. The concrete floor beneath me was cold and wet. I laid my head against my knees, dejected and scared of what was to come.

Anything was better than being here. But at the same time, I wasn't ready to mate with a pack. They could take a second omega anytime after buying me. I didn't have anything going for me now. No job, no family. *Why would they even like me?*

The next morning, I woke up with a pit in my stomach. My life was about to change drastically, and I had no control over what would happen. My room was still dark, with barely any sunlight coming through the dingy window. Slowly getting up, I walked to the bathroom and brushed my teeth. I was moving on autopilot. Refusing to think about my fate.

When I walked back into my room, my dad stood there carrying a dress. I gasped, recognizing it as my mom's dress. Ever since she died, he had never allowed me to go into their room or touch Mom's stuff.

It was her dark plum dress made of velvet. It was heavy and warm to wear in the fall.

"Wear this," he said. He had zero emotion in his voice, his eyes a dead stare. "Put on some makeup too. We're leaving in ten minutes."

I looked at my worn-out mattress and saw that he had thrown some of my mom's makeup on it. It didn't shock me that he couldn't care less about what would happen to me since would just bring him money to fund his lifestyle. I shut the door behind him.

When I lifted Mom's dress, I burst into tears like a flood waiting to break.

Tears flowed freely down my face, drenching the dress. I knelt on the ground, hugging the dress to my heart, inhaling Mom's scent. It still had her flowery perfume that I loved when I snuggled up against her.

I felt numb as each tear dripped down my face. I sat there, rocking back and forth, holding her dress to my heart. I missed her so much. Her laughter and her stories. She loved to read, and I'd always go into her room, where sometimes she'd read aloud to me when I was a child.

"What do I do, Mom?" I whispered.

I sat there, hopeless and lost. The only thing of comfort was the dress. The only nice thing my father ever did since she died was to give me her dress. Staying in this house any longer with my father was unbearable. It was time to leave, whether it was through an auction or not. And that was the motivation I needed.

It was now or never. I slowly stood up and changed into the dress. It was a bit tight since Mom was more petite than I was, but the length was good.

In the bathroom, I washed my face and combed out my long hair-allowing the waves from yesterday to fall down my shoulders. Then, I used Mom's makeup, dabbing on purple eyeshadow to match the dress. I was pretty sure the makeup was expired, but that was all I had—no time to be picky.

"Are you done yet?" my dad called, appearing at the bathroom door. He wore a beige suit that made his skin look blotchy and gross.

"Yes, I think so. I just have to take the pills now," I said. The two heat suppressants and the scent blocker. "Last night, I didn't take any."

He might've forgotten with all the auction excitement.

"I threw them away," he said with an evil smile. "You have to be as appealing as possible to the buyers. No refunds."

What?! Without the heat suppressants, I could go into heat at anytime and I would need a pack of alphas to have sex with during my fertile time. It would be dangerous if I went into heat. Without a knot from an alpha, an omega could sick and eventually go unconscious- in some cases, even die. I couldn't believe I was under the mercy of the alpha pack who would purchase me.

It was noon by the time we drove to the Omega Auction. The place was so far out it was nearly an hour's drive. I couldn't believe my eyes when I saw signs saying the next auction was starting at noon. I had never been to one of these auctions, because I had no reason to be here.

But it was still the norm for leftover omegas to be sold, especially for poorer families who didn't have many options.

My dad drove around to the back of a building.

"We're here. If you embarrass me at all, you're dead," he threatened, looking over at me as he unbuckled his seat belt.

I didn't say anything as I stepped out of the car. I vowed to never talk to him again after today. We walked towards the open door in the back, and I watched as my dad greeted the bald auctioneer. The auctioneer was holding a measuring tape and a clipboard fussing around but stopped when he saw me walk in.

"I'd like to put my daughter up for auction," my dad stated matter-of-factly. Like the auction was an everyday thing. This was going to be seared into my memory forever. The auctioneer looked at me like I was an object as he measured my breasts and my waist over my dress.

"Perfect. She will bring in some money," the auctioneer said. "Now, let's get you over to the makeup guy. Your purple eyeshadow is atrocious."

Before I knew it, I was seated next to ten other omegas with families fussing excitedly over them. Like this was the best thing to ever happen to them. I was confused and baffled by all of this. But I noticed that the families barely had any clothes on, some with their sandals ripped in many places covered in sand from the island.

We were in a large studio, getting prepped before they took us outside to the stage. My dad was chatting loudly with a few other alphas as he watched me with hawkish eyes, ensuring I complied and didn't run away.

I *did* want to run away, but there was nowhere to hide in Howl's Edge.

The makeup artist wearing a floral shirt approached me and immediately started drenching my face in foundation. I closed my eyes, hating every moment of it. I didn't need all that makeup and was sure I'd look like a clown at the end of it. As I sat there with my eyes closed, I thought about my mom and what she would say if she saw this. She would tell me to have fun and roll with it- that things will always get better.

I smiled slightly, thinking of how optimistic she was while I was the total opposite.

"Ooh, la la. Look in the mirror. You look amazing," said the make-up artist with a flourish, waving his hand to the mirror in front of me. My eyes widened when I caught my reflection in the mirror. He had accentuated my features with gold eyeshadow, making my eyes look seductive with his color choices.

"Oh wow," I whispered, pressing my plump red lips together.

It was time for the auction, and it was sweltering outside. My mom's thick velvet dress did nothing to help with the heat. I was chained by the ankle to two other omegas on either side of me. The purple-haired omega to my right looked miserable and kept flicking the crowd off with her middle finger.

"What are you doing?" I whispered.

"Lowering my value," she smirked. "It's how I was passed up on the last two auctions. No one wants a badly behaved omega."

"I might have to take a page out of your book," I muttered. I didn't have the guts to flick off an entire crowd of alphas, and my dad was eagerly watching from the back. The omega on my other side was nervous, sweat beading down her forehead, constantly biting her fingernails. I squinted in the sun, looking out at the small crowd of buyers who had started shouting prices at the auctioneer.

They were going down the line, and I was almost next.

As I looked at the buyers, I saw groups of alphas in packs. Some were leering and gazing at us with lustful gazes. Ugh, this was going to be horrible. I felt sorry for the omega who ended up with a creepy buyer. Then, my eyes stopped on a familiar patch of white silver hair.

He looked up, and my heart nearly stopped. It was Jatix. What the hell was *he* doing here?

I thought we had an amazing time at the ball, but I thought we had a connection. A little bit of sadness flowed through me. *Why was he here?* Maybe he was looking for a maid to press his fancy suits.

He looked in my direction, and instantly our gazes locked on one another. My heart started beating erratically. I shook my head to convey to him that he shouldn't purchase me. I didn't want him. He had met me when I was a doctor, and now I was in an auction. It was way too humiliating, and I didn't want to explain how I got into this situation.

He smiled softly with pity in his eyes, and I quickly looked away.

I was trapped here, chained to other omegas, and it was soon going to be my turn to be put up.

Chapter 8

Jatix

I knew exactly who I wanted.

This was the last place I expected the cute omega doctor to be. My soul lifted, and every look we shared made my dick dance.

"It's her," whispered Darius beside me. I knew she affected him the same way by the way he looked at her, awestruck.

"What the fuck is she doing here?" I said out loud. She looked away from me, and I caught her slight headshake. *Did she not want me? Why was she evading me?*

"No idea."

We had been talking about this omega ever since we had both seen her at the ball. I was glad Darius saw her for himself. He understood the allure that I was talking about. I couldn't stop talking about her until Silus was fed up with me. She looked absolutely splendid standing up on that stage. *Who the fuck would put her up for auction?* She wasn't ugly in any way, and she was an accomplished omega. I didn't understand.

But I knew one thing.

There was no way in hell I'd let another alpha purchase her. She was going to be mine. I was going to fight tooth and nail for that girl.

She was scared, and her eyes darted nervously toward me every once in a while. She was nowhere close to the funny, spicy girl I had met yesterday with the quick wit. Her demeanor was off today. It was as if she had reached a breaking point in her life. I vowed to myself that I would do everything in my power to learn everything about her. And to make her happy.

"Up next. Keera!" shouted the auctioneer, walking over to her on stage. He waved his hat towards her, bringing attention to her ample breasts. "The bidding starts!"

"One thousand!" someone called out.

"Three thousand!" said another.

"Six thousand!" I roared. But it didn't end there. It was fierce, and the alphas kept making the bids higher and higher until I shouted, "twenty-five thousand!"

Everyone gasped, and the auctioneer looked around to see if anyone else had a counteroffer.

"Going once! Going twice! Sold to the Lustfur Pack!" said the auctioneer, untying the chains around Keera's ankles. "That was the biggest sale in five years, I have to say."

Yes, she was mine now under the law- there was no way I would lose her this time.

Chapter 9

Keera

I couldn't believe it.

I was officially sold, and I was shaking while the auctioneer removed the chain from my ankle. I didn't know how to feel about this. Suddenly, I felt like my thoughts and actions weren't mine anymore. I was someone's property. I could smell my orange scent as I was sweating profusely.

"Congratulations! You're part of the Lustfur Pack," said the auctioneer, walking me down the stage towards my new pack.

"Thanks," I said sarcastically as I was forced to meet my new pack. I recognized the Delta bodyguard at the ball. He was standing next to Jatix. I couldn't look at Jatix in the eyes as I approached them. I had no idea what he was thinking about me. He probably thought I was some pathetic omega unloved by her family.

Which *was* partly true.

"Good job, daughter," said my dad, who followed me. I knew he was ultimately waiting for his money. I watched as Jatix handed over a wad of cash to the auctioneer, who took a portion for himself and most of it to my dad.

"Any parting words for your daughter?" asked the auctioneer, looking between us.

"Actually, I do. Do you mind if I steal her for a minute?" my dad requested.

Yes, I mind! What the fuck did he want?

"Not at all," said Jatix, pushing me with the small of my back towards my dad. "Say goodbye to your dad. You'll have the rest of your life with me after today."

He winked, and I rolled my eyes.

Reluctantly, I followed my dad toward the back of the building.

Once we were out of sight of everyone, he immediately wrapped his fingers around my throat. My eyes bugged in shock as I struggled to pull away. I opened my mouth to scream, but I couldn't breathe as he blocked my airflow.

"If you dare tell anyone about how I treated you, I will hunt you down," he threatened, spittle flying in my face. His angry little mustache was red in the sun. "I will personally kill you myself and avenge my wife."

I was slowly losing oxygen, and my throat was constricted. My vision was swimming as I began to lose consciousness.

"Release her!" roared a male voice. I couldn't see who it was. But within seconds, my father was pulled off me and pinned against his car. I wheezed, gasping in little breaths at a time. I put a hand to my throat, trying to massage the pain.

Jatix's arm flexed as he squeezed my father's throat. I have never seen his eyes glow such an electric purple. He was angry. The delta guard stood beside him, flexing his muscles, ready to finish the job.

"Stop, no," I said, running towards Jatix, grabbing his forearm.

"I can kill him for you right here," Jatix spat. Then he released him, and my father fumbled with his keys to get in the car. Then he took off.

"Does he always treat you like this?" asked Jatix.

"No, not really. He's just sad I'm leaving," I said.

I didn't know why I was protecting my dad. I just wanted to leave quietly without any drama.

"That's not how sad looks," said Jatix.

"Disgusting," said the delta guard shaking his head and flexing his shoulders. I didn't say anything as we stood silently, listening to the auctioneer yell out numbers to the crowd for the next round of omegas. I watched my dad's car zoom away and sighed in relief. This would be the last time I'd ever see him.

Anyone was better than him.

"Are you okay?" asked Jatix, walking over to me and placing his fingers on my neck, and I flinched. He immediately pulled his fingers back. "He left purple marks on you. The bastard."

"It's okay," I said lightly, biting my lip. His jaw twitched with hidden anger. It was no big deal though, I was used to people getting angry at me. "Are you mad at me?"

"No darling," he said quickly. "I'm angry at your father. You don't deserve to be treated this way. Do you know that?"

"I know," I said, my voice small.

"Kind of odd meeting you here," said Jatix. I looked up, determined to show that I was strong despite what he had just witnessed.

"It's odd seeing *you* here," I countered, trying to make him forget my moment of weakness. "How could you purchase omegas like they're objects?"

Only the worst alphas would be here. He looked taken aback by my accusation, his purple eyes flashing. His bodyguard's jaw flexed like I hit a nerve. The bodyguard wasn't looking at me at all. What the hell was *his* problem?

"I wasn't going to let some other alpha buy you," said Jatix, slowly and evenly. "Would you have preferred to end up with a different pack?"

"Are you saying that you knew I'd be here?"

"No," said Jatix. "Let's get out of here. It's hot as fuck. And fix that attitude, little kitten."

"I don't want to go with you," I said brazenly, planting my heels into the ground.

Jatix smiled widely. "Do you want to do this the easy way or the hard way? I can have Darius carry you to the car. Would you like everyone to take a good look at your bottom? Because that's only for me and my pack, but I'm willing to share."

"Fine," I said. "I'll walk."

Fuming, I walked alongside Jatix as he led me to his sleek silver sportscar. He opened the passenger door, and I carefully sat inside, scared to mess up the upholstery. It looked like it was brand new. He buckled me in, and my breath caught when his hands brushed against the front of my chest. I wasn't prepared for the tingle of warmth between my legs. *What the hell?* One day off the pills, and I was already feeling horny.

His peppermint scent was heaven to my nose as he leaned closer, buckling in the seatbelt. His rough hand pressed against my thigh. As I pressed my thighs together, I felt slick drenching me between my legs. My orange scent was thick and heavy without my scent blockers. I hoped my arousal wouldn't cloud my judgment. If he wanted to mate me tonight, I would be alright with it, but it was my omega instincts talking.

Jatix seemed to sense it as well.

"I can smell you," he said, still leaning down over me, closing his eyes, and breathing deeply. I tried to close my legs tighter, but that caused even more slick to drench my panties. "Can't wait to taste."

His comment caused my pussy to clench as he gazed at me. Then he closed the door, and Darius jumped into the backseat, missing the entire interaction. I tried to regain my breath when Jatix entered the driver's seat. My pulse was racing so fast. *Did he say he wanted to taste me?* My fantasies were running wild at this point.

"So, what do you intend to do with me?" I asked him.

He turned to me as he drove, "to love you, mate you and breed you. What else?"

My eyebrows rose at his frank answer.

"I still want a job and to put my doctorate into doing useful stuff," I said.

"Of course," he said. "I have no plans to stifle your goals."

"Do you plan on taking whatever money I make?"

"Whatever money you make is your own. What kind of alpha do you think I am?" Jatix looked insulted as he stared into the sandy roads and palm trees covering the island, his eyebrows furrowed.

"Sorry," I said.

He looked over at me again. "Hey, it's okay. I know you're scared. Omegas don't have much power in Howl's Edge, but it could happen one day."

"What do you expect out of me in this relationship?" I asked.

"As I said, make love constantly and make babies. I'm looking for something long-term," he answered without a hint of sarcasm. His face actually looked serious for once. "By the way, that's Darius back there. He'll be making love to you too."

I almost gasped at how blasé and relaxed he sounded saying that. I couldn't imagine taking in Darius. He looked huge. I started to squirm in my seat, thinking about it. Thoughts of their naked bodies pressed against mine, desperate to get me pregnant. I squeezed my thighs tighter, trying to dispel the naughty thoughts plaguing my mind.

"Oh, I thought he was your bodyguard," I said.

"I told you to get a beta," grumbled Darius from the backseat. His voice was a deep rumble. "Omegas think they're too good for us deltas."

"No," I said, trying to rectify my mistake. "That's not what I meant at all."

Jatix laughed, parking the car in front of a mansion of a house. I gaped at it, shocked at how massive it was.

"Let's go. Time to introduce you to the rest of my delightful little pack," said Jatix.

Stepping out of the car, I couldn't tear my eyes away from how big this house was. It stood on the ocean side, palm trees lining the pathway to the front door. It was picturesque.

As we walked inside, I took in the beautiful staircase and the spacious white living room. I couldn't imagine having little babies running around here. It was spotless, and everything was made out of glass. The first person I saw was in the kitchen. He had brown shaggy hair and glasses as he stirred a pot. He had a wideset body and a little bit of a belly.

"I have a surprise," called Jatix. "Our new omega is here!"

The chubbier alpha smiled widely and quickly made his way over to me. He shook my hand enthusiastically, and my face cracked into the first smile of the day. He exuded joy and energy that was infectious.

"It's so nice to meet you finally," he gushed. "Jatix couldn't stop talking about how beautiful you were after the Omega Ball last night."

"It's nice to meet you too," I said when he pulled me in for a giant hug. I decided I liked him the most already.

"I'm Shawn. Let me introduce you to my twin, Silus. He's somewhere outside working out," said Shawn.

"No need, I'm here," said another male voice, entering the back door. Shawn's twin looked almost identical to him, except for the enormous amount of tattoos he had on his body. Even more tattoos than Darius. He walked over to me and took my hand, bringing it to his lips. "I'm Silus."

"I'm Keera. Nice to meet you," I said. I could tell that Silus and Shawn were alphas from their thick scents of oakwood. Darius's scent was more lowkey, and I only caught whiffs of it when he was right next to me.

"You're beautiful," Silus said without hesitation. "If Jatix is too much, let me know."

"How am I ever too much?" asked Jatix, with a shocked look on his face. "Am I too much Keera, my love?"

60

I smiled, and the men guffawed.

"Just a little bit," I said.

"Let me show you to your room," said Jatix. Then he looked at my backpack, which had barely anything in it. "Is that all you have?"

"Yes," I said.

"Soon, you have to tell us about your family. You are one big mystery to me," said Jatix, leading me up the stairs.

"It's nothing interesting," I said. "My mother died when I was sixteen, and my father raised me."

"Why did he put you up for auction?"

"We were poor, and our house was going into foreclosure," I said, my lines rehearsed at my father's insistence during the long car ride to the Omega Auction. The last thing he wanted was the law to come after him for omega mistreatment.

"I see," he replied, walking down the hallway when we reached upstairs. "This is your room."

I looked inside and gasped.

There was a bed. An actual alpha-sized bed sitting in the middle of the room. And on the other side of the room, there were curtains sectioning it off from the rest of the room in a round circle. My heart was pounding with anticipation as I pulled back the sheer curtains.

There was a pink circle mattress with pink blankets and sheets. It was a little omega nest. Complete with books in a pile next to it and candles.

"Is this...is this for me?" I asked. I was too scared to ask in case it wasn't.

"Yes. Do you think any of us would be able to fit in there?" replied Jatix. "But yes, anytime you need to relax and be alone, this is yours."

I couldn't believe it. I didn't want to believe that they were being so nice to me.

"Cool," I said dismissively if they were all messing with me. Everything was happening too quickly, too fast.

"You also have your own bathroom in here, complete with a shower," said Jatix, opening the bathroom door near the room's entrance. He looked slightly disappointed that I wasn't gushing with joy.

Inside I was flipping out with excitement, but I didn't want to show it.

"Oh wow," I said, walking into the bathroom. It was spacious and looked like it was bleached inside and out. The toilet and sink were white, and the bathtub looked like it had never been touched. There were even little pink bathroom slippers sitting next to the door.

"Shawn made sure to get those slippers," said Jatix. "To match your nest."

"I'll make sure to thank him," I said. Regardless of how many things they threw at me, I still couldn't trust all this. I couldn't trust him completely and let my guard down. Because at any time, my heart could get broken.

All the luxury in the world wasn't going to mend a broken omega's heart.

Chapter 10

Jatix

"I'm going to take a quick shower now if you don't mind," said Keera, waiting for me to leave.

The problem was...I wasn't going to just *leave*. She couldn't get rid of me, just like that.

I let out a soft chuckle.

"Tsk tsk," I said. "You will have one of us bathing you and touching every part of your body during your showers. My pack and I will not get denied the pleasures of our omega."

Her eyes widened, and her pale cheeks reddened under all her makeup. I could tell she was uncomfortable by the way her eyes shifted to the door. At the same time, her body was perfuming in her excitement. I could smell her sweet thick orange scent get stronger by the minute. *Oh, I couldn't wait to get a taste of that pussy*. She was going to know who I was.

And she was going to know that soon enough.

"I can shower by myself," she said, crossing her arms across her ripe breasts.

God, she looked so damn cute. Her black hair was messy around her red face as she glared at me. Her perfect mascara was smeared under her eyelids. I wanted to scoop her up and kiss her petulant lips.

"That's not how it works, sweetheart," I said. "It will create a closer bond between alpha and omega. You need to get used to my touch. Go ahead and strip off your clothes. Everything off."

It looked like she regretted mentioning her shower to me as she slowly and deliberately lifted her purple dress over her head. My cock hardened as I gazed at her body. She only had a thick pair of black cotton panties and a white bra. After her shower, I was definitely going to provide her with sexier things to wear. She would be a mated omega soon, and it was time to grow up.

I started to remove my suit, which was stifling. Throwing my tie on the ground, I watched Keera from the side of my eyes as she slowly pulled down her panties. She didn't think I was watching her as I removed my pants and briefs next. She was the most skittish omega I've ever met, and it was necessary for her to get used to me.

I gazed at her naked body.

She covered the dark patch between her legs with her hand, leaving her breasts free. Her breasts look like moon orbs, begging to be caressed. Her nipples were hard pink pebbles. Her waist was slim, her thighs and butt voluptuous. Her musky orange scent intensified in the room with her clothes off.

I stood in front of her, sniffing the air deeply. Drunk off her scent.

I headed into the shower, turned on the water, and adjusted the temperature. When the powerful shower head came to life, I offered her my hand, and we both climbed into the tub. The hot water soaked her hair first, and she turned towards the water, her back facing me.

Even though she tried to avoid me, I didn't mind. Her butt looked delicious.

I squirted soap into a white loofah and slowly rubbed her shoulders. She silently lifted her hair and leaned to the side, allowing her neck to relax as I pressed her shoulders with the loofah, covering her with bubbly white soap. When I caught sight of the pink marks on her neck from her father choking her, white-hot rage filled me. I closed my eyes and took a deep breath as I washed her shoulders gently.

I would deal with that prick later. *Was her father always like this? Did she have to put up with that ass her whole life?* I needed to ask her and find out everything about her. She acted like she had her shit together, but it was slowly unraveling. I wanted to get to know the *real* Keera.

I washed her back next, swirling the loofah downwards, stopping at the curve of her amazing buttocks. I threw the loofah to the side, using my bare hands to wash her lower back, and I heard her intake of breath. When my hand made contact with her skin, it felt like an electric shock between us. My cock was hard as fuck under the stream of water as I washed her bottom next.

"Bend down, sweetie," I commanded. "I need to wash between those beautiful cheeks of yours."

"I can wash that myself," she tried to protest. But I pressed her back gently, and she obeyed. Her orange scent, like thick perfume, permeated my nose as she bent down. I had to stop myself from ramming my cock deep inside her pink pussy until she could taste it.

I maneuvered to her side and grasped her right breast with one hand and my other hand holding her bottom. My cock was swinging in her face, but I didn't care.

I wanted her to know how she affected me. She had to get used to it.

"I'm going to wash that sweet ass," I said. "Spread your legs, honey."

She spread her legs, and my fingers slipped between her crack. I rubbed my fingers up and down, feeling her secret ridges. Her dark hole. I squirted soap into my hand and washed her anus in circles with my thumb as I squeezed her breast. Her scent thickened in the steamy shower the more I rubbed her bottom.

I patted her butt.

"All done?" she asked breathlessly.

"Yes, good girl. Let's get your front washed," I said, spinning her around. She stood in front of me, her hair plastered to her pink face and down her shoulders. She gripped my shoulders as I began to swirl the loofah over each of her moon breasts. Her pink nipples hardened, the ends of them dripping with water. I wanted to take them in my mouth so badly.

But it wasn't time.

She needed to get used to my touch first. At the same time, she looked impatient as she jutted her chest out further- taunting me. I knew she wanted more but was too prideful to say anything.

I rubbed the loofah down to her belly, large soapy bubbles seeping down to her pubic hair covering her pussy. I dropped the loofah again and washed the outside of her vagina with my hand. In my head, I imagined kneeling and spreading her open under my tongue.

My finger slipped inside her pussy, feeling her slick from inside. Her slick signified how ready she was for me.

"When is your next heat?" I asked.

"I never went through one," she said. "I've used heat suppressants my whole life."

"Are you taking them now?"

"No."

"Good," I said, pressing my finger further up inside her, and her eyes rolled back in her head. She was enjoying this. "Are you a virgin?"

"I think so...not really," she stuttered, trying to get away from my finger, distracted by my question. Like it was something bad. I removed my finger, confused why the question seemed to trigger her.

"That's okay," I said. "I'd prefer you not to be a virgin for all the activities I have planned for you."

"What activities?" she asked as I rubbed soap over her thick thighs.

"It's a surprise," I said.

"Why do you like teasing me?" she asked with a sly smile. The sparkle back in her eyes. The awkward moment earlier, forgotten for now. But I swore to myself I was going to dig deeper. I had to know what was going on. *What was she hiding?*

"I want you to beg for my cock, little missy. It gets me off."

"How about my turn to tease you?" she asked, grabbing the loofah from the bathtub floor. I smirked as she squirted soap into it. She brushed the loofah over my biceps with a look of concentration. Her little pink tongue sticking out. "You look like you're thin, but without your clothes, I can see all your muscles."

I flexed my muscles, annoyed at being called thin.

"Looks like I'll have to spend more time working out with Silus," I grumbled.

She rubbed the loofah over my chest, licking her lips. "You're so tall. You're a lot of man to handle."

Okay, that fixed my bruised ego. *Just a little.* When she lowered herself to my navel, my breath hitched. My cock hardened and waved at her. I wondered what she was going to do with it. Instead, I watched as her eyes widened while she stared at my hard cock.

She slowly rubbed the loofah over it.

"I prefer your hand over the loofah," I gently encouraged. "Don't be scared of it, sweetheart."

Even though she wasn't a virgin, she acted like she had never seen a dick before. Maybe she had horrible sex with a beta or something.

"Okay," she whispered, using her bare hand instead, gripping it between her fingers. "It's long and thick."

"Oh, is it?" I said, egging her on. My cock was getting harder, and I had to stop myself from thrusting eagerly into her hand.

"Can I taste it?"

"Yes, oh my god," I said. I was fucking suffering as she slowly licked the tip. "Take my cock into your sweet little pink mouth." I leaned my hand against the shower wall for balance as she pulled my cock into her mouth. I was weak against her touch.

"Like this?" she asked, her voice muffled against my cock as she took it in. My cock twitched again, ready to burst.

"Go up and down, sweetie," I said. My eyes were closed as I tried not to thrust into her mouth. *Don't scare her.* All of a sudden, she swirled the tip of my cock with her tongue and expertly pulled my cock into her mouth, going up and down. Her hot mouth was tight around my dick as she milked it between her lips.

I didn't last five seconds before I exploded.

She tried to swallow, but it was too much semen.

I spurted all over the bath floor as she finished me off with her hand. I nearly collapsed from the powerful orgasm she just gave me. She continued washing my legs with the loofah nonchalantly.

"Do you feel satisfied, my alpha?" she asked with a wink. Droplets of water flowed beautifully down her hair and shoulders.

"Wait, you acted all innocent around my dick," I said. "You know your way around a cock, don't you? So you were teasing me the whole time?"

"I wasn't living under a rock," she giggled. "I said I'd tease you back, remember?"

She stood up, and I couldn't help but grab her face between my hands. Her dark eyelashes fluttered closed as she lifted her face to me. I leaned in and captured her lips, kissing her under the hot shower. My dreams of her finally coming true.

Chapter 11

Shawn

"They've been in that shower awhile now," I said, trying to hear what was going on with my keen alpha hearing as I put together spaghetti sauce for our pasta dinner tonight.

"J is clearly working his magic in the shower. Hope he gets some pussy," laughed Silus, leaning against the island table in the kitchen. "What do you think, Darius?"

Darius was flipping through the channels on the TV.

"He's unpredictable. Who knows what's happening," grumbled Darius.

"Damn, I wish it was me in that shower with her," I said, shaking my head. She smelled so amazing. Like oranges.

Having dinner with an omega was going to be refreshing, and I couldn't wait. Watching her eat would turn me on like crazy. I loved watching females eat.

Jatix had taken a hiatus from dating, and we all had to suffer along with him. He didn't care about relationships in the past, and we were allowed to screw whoever showed up at the door. But ever since he saw the Frostcrown Pack happy with their omega, he wanted the same, even though he never admitted it outright.

"I don't think the omega gives a shit about us," said Silus.

"Why so negative?" I asked, stirring the huge pot. My twin brother could be such a pessimist.

"She was bought at an auction. The worst place," he drawled, leaning his head against his hand. "I need to test her somehow. Figure out her true intentions."

"You should be a little trusting," I advised. "You're going to make her hate us."

Silus rolled his eyes like I was being naive.

"Jatix had a proposal from King Saku at the ball," said Darius.

"The king wanted to marry J?" asked Silus, smirking.

"No, you fucker. He wanted Princess Lyra to marry Jatix," growled Darius.

"What the hell did J say?"

"He refused. We would have been tied to the Royal Pack if he accepted," said Darius.

"Fuck, we would have been royalty," said Silus. "But Keera is hotter, so it doesn't matter. I just have to figure out if she's for real."

"Just get to know this omega. Even though she comes from an auction, it doesn't mean she's any less than a normal omega," I stressed. "You watch. She may be the greatest thing that ever happens to us."

Chapter 12

Keera

As I slathered on lotion in the bathroom, I couldn't help but grin a little at my brazenness of sucking an alpha's cock for the first time. I didn't know what took over me in the shower, but his presence pulled me to him. Called to my darkest senses like nothing I was ever used to.

Jatix had left to give me some space, and I finally felt like I had some privacy. The ache between my legs increased as I blow-dried my hair, thinking about what happened in the shower. Jatix mentioned going downstairs for dinner, so I wanted to look presentable.

I still wasn't sure what to feel about all of this.

This was officially the pack that I was sold to. *Did they think less of me since I was put up for auction?* I felt self-conscious as I sifted through the outfits in the closet. I wanted something elegant to wear tonight. Three alphas and one delta would be watching my every move tonight. I had always wanted to be in a pack that adored me. I just never thought it would ever be in the cards for me. Every time an omega gave birth at Howl's Honor Hospital, I would be reminded of what I was missing. But sometimes, I'd see a pack that wasn't so nice to their omega, and I would feel bad for the omega.

I wasn't sure if the pack would like me in this case. I didn't understand how I had kissed Jatix already, but he was an insistent alpha who never took no for an answer. Even though Jatix was pretty odd, I started falling for him against my better judgment. The shower kiss was epic, and it left me panting for more. Or maybe I was naïve. My omega instincts were emerging without my heat suppressants. I've never felt so many emotions at once, especially the arousal strumming through my belly and squeezing my belly.

I looked in the long mirror next to the nest they had assembled for me. I wore a thin white summer dress that wasn't too fancy for a simple dinner. It was strapless, and the dress stopped right above my knees. I hoped it didn't look too slutty. I spent forever in this closet trying to pick something to wear. I'm sure they wouldn't care what I wore as long as I was naked. I needed to stop freaking out. I had carefully hung my mother's dress safely in the back of the closet.

I looked over at the nest in the corner, and I hesitantly made my way to it.

Pulling the curtain aside, I put my hand to my mouth as I softly gasped again as I gazed at how cute it was. I stepped in and stood on the bed in my bare feet. The mattress was so squishy and soft under my feet. Nothing like the thin paper I slept on at home. I slowly lowered myself and sat on the mattress. It felt like clouds under my body. I used to have a normal bed before Mom died. After she died, my dad frantically threw away anything that made me comfortable, and I never understood why.

"Oh my god," I whispered as I lay on it. Then, as I slowly got more comfortable, my eyes drifted closed. The pink blankets were absolutely divine and cozy. Pulling it around me, I hugged the blankets tightly, scenting them with my omega perfume.

It was too good to be true as I absorbed the beautiful sensation I had been deprived of for years.

Darius

"Find her Darius. Tell Keera it's dinner time," said Jatix as he set down the plates. Judging from the look of contentment on his face, I could tell he had a fantastic time in the shower with our brand new omega.

I wanted that.

I was jealous. That was for fucking sure.

"Yeah," I said, lifting my ass from the couch. It had been a long day in the sun this morning at the auction, and I was about ready to pass out. A flutter of excitement hit my belly as I walked up the stairs. Even though I disliked omegas, I couldn't squash the hope that went through me. I swiped my hand through my hair as I stood outside her door. I couldn't hear anything inside.

I knocked softly.

No answer.

Did she fucking escape out the window? I knew this would fucking happen.

I quickly turned the doorknob and burst into the room like a wild beast. I was about to shout her name until I saw her body curled up in the nest. I could see her outline through the sheer pink curtains.

She was sleeping in the nest we made.

I felt like a fool bursting in there and suddenly felt terrible if I had woken her. I walked as quietly as possible towards her nest and pulled the curtain back. My heart softened as I gazed at her sleeping face. She was all bundled up in the blankets we had carefully picked out for her.

And it warmed my heart to see that.

She looked so cute, and I only wanted to lay beside her. Hug her and absorb her orange scent. I knelt next to her and stared into her face before I had to wake her up for dinner. Upon closer inspection, her face looked troubled. Her eyelids were trembling, and tears were pouring down her cheeks. Panicking, I quickly tried to wake her up by shaking her shoulder.

"Wake up, Keera, it's dinner time," I mumbled.

Her eyes shot open, and they were red. She looked at me, horrified, and my heart sank. Omegas didn't like deltas. That was a fact of life. They only loved alphas. But then she was blubbering something, still staring at me, her eyes unmoving. She began screaming, and I realized she was still in a dream world.

"No, get away!" she screamed, punching an invisible person in front of her. Her eyes were still glazed over.

"Keera, wake up," I said more firmly, shaking her arm. When she finally came to, she was breathing hard and looked at me with fresh eyes.

"Oh, Darius," she gasped. "I'm sorry. I had a nightmare."

I was relieved she didn't hate me as she scooted over to me and laid her head against my chest. My heart ached for her. I protectively wrapped my arms around her as we sat in her nest. *What in the world had she gone through?* Was she dreaming about her father? I was going to kill that bastard without her knowing.

I rumbled deep in my chest to soothe her. To calm her racing heart and she leaned into me for strength, wrapping her arms around my waist. Her tears soaked through my white shirt, but I didn't give a fuck about my shirt getting a little wet.

This little omega was going through something that I didn't know. My purring was soothing her, at least. She stopped crying, and her breathing returned to normal. Her omega scent was no longer laced with stark fear.

"What were you dreaming about?" I asked slowly.

"I can't talk about it," she whimpered. "I think I'm too damaged to be here."

"No, you're not," I said, confused she would say such a thing. I rubbed her back as she shuddered. "You're not damaged at all sweetheart."

"What makes you so sure?"

"No one can be more damaged than Jatix," I said, trying to comfort her.

She curiously pulled away to look at me. I wiped her tears with the pad of my thumb.

"Why? What happened to him?" she asked.

"He was born to a psycho-alpha mother. She didn't want a child with white hair, so she made his life a living hell," I explained. "I'll let Jatix tell you the specifics, but I'll leave it at that for now."

Alpha females were notorious for being tough and not so very nurturing. They were the no-nonsense type.

"Poor Jatix," she said, her brows furrowed in worry.

"Everyone has a dark past somewhere," I said.

"What's yours?"

"Well, for one, omegas never liked me," I admitted. "Back in college, an omega girl pretended to like me to the amusement of her friends. The day she broke my heart was the worst. Ever since then, I stayed far away from omegas."

"I would never do that to you," said Keera in earnest, her scent rising. My mouth quirked up in a smile.

"We'll see. I came up here to call you for dinner."

"Oh," she exclaimed, slapping her forehead. "I'm sorry I fell asleep."

"It's okay," I said, hearing her stomach growl. *Fuck*, she was cute. She was going to be my weak spot, I was sure of it. If anyone ever hurt her, so help me god. And if I *ever* saw her father again, he wouldn't live another day. After what I had seen at the auction today, he wasn't one of the good guys. He was the type of guy I would hunt down in the streets to kill. "Are you ready to meet the rest of the pack?"

"Yes," she said eagerly, a small smile on her face.

Chapter 13

Keera

Darius followed behind me as I walked down the stairs, my hand on the gold handrail. It was cool and smooth under my palm. The house was magnificent with its open structure and tall ceilings.

"She's here," I heard Jatix say in a singsong voice. Jatix was dangerous to trust, but I started falling for him. My little omega heart wanted to mate with him, but I had to pull the reins on it.

"Hi," I said, stopping just outside the kitchen. Silus was sitting at the dining table, and Jatix was gathering forks. I wasn't sure about Silus. He seemed distant and a little bit cold towards me.

Darius stood next to me protectively, his body close to mine.

"Come in!" said the one named Shawn in a booming voice.

"Am I allowed into the kitchen?" I asked. All the men stopped what they were doing, staring at me open-mouthed. *Oh shit*, did I say something wrong? I hope I didn't piss them off so early already.

"Yes, of course," said Shawn, looking at me with wide eyes as he carried the pot of spaghetti to the table. "Were you never allowed to go into the kitchen before?"

"My dad said it would bring out my nesting instincts," I said quickly, like it was common sense. But apparently, it wasn't.

"Did he allow you to have a bed?" asked Jatix slowly. There was pressure in his voice, tension, and anger. I knew it was weird the way I lived. But I thought most omegas had to live the way I did.

"Well, not exactly. But I had a mattress, though," I said.

"Blankets?" Darius pressed, cracking his knuckles.

Fear spiked through me at the intensity of the men around me. My omega nature wanted them to be calm. Naturally, an omega's job was to please her alpha.

"No," I whispered, staring hard at the vase of roses on the table. I wanted to look anywhere but at them. Without the pills, I could smell my orange scent permeating the room, getting stronger with my shame.

"There's no reason for you to feel ashamed of anything," said Shawn, sensing my energy. He pulled a chair out. "Come and sit."

Grateful to do something than stand there in front of their watchful gazes, I sat between Silus and Darius at the dining table. The last time I had a proper meal with a family was a long time ago. The tomatoes and oregano wafted in the air as Jatix poured a heapful of pasta on a plate for me. I grabbed a fork and began digging in.

It tasted like heaven itself. The first bite melted on my tongue.

"Wow, Shawn, you can cook. Very tasty," I said around a mouthful of pasta. Shawn was watching me with satisfaction in his eyes, barely touching his plate. It made me feel a little self-conscious but also caused tendrils of arousal to rise in me.

"Thanks, Keera. I enjoy cooking," said Shawn. "It's my profession during the day, actually. Doesn't do well for my belly, though." He tapped his belly, and I smiled.

"And it doesn't help me either," said Silus. "This pasta is going to slow me down during my workout later. Why couldn't you make something healthy?"

"Why don't you fucking cook then?" said Shawn, waving his fork around threateningly. I couldn't help but smile at the twins' exchange. They were twins but so different in every way. While Silus liked to stay in shape and covered in tattoos- Shawn was more domestic and lighthearted. Silus was intense every time he looked my way, and when I met his gaze, I was always the first to look away. I didn't understand Silus yet and had no idea what went through his mind. Jatix was more transparent. His dark, lustful gazes assured me that he wanted me in every way, causing my thighs to clench in arousal.

The dining room was quiet as everyone slurped up the pasta, devouring the food. The clink of forks upon plates was the only sound apart from all the chewing and grunting of the males.

Jatix cleared his throat and wiped his mouth with a napkin.

"Tomorrow will be the introduction ceremony," he announced, gently setting his napkin down.

"What's that?" I asked.

"We are going to explore every crevice of your body," he said like it was something normal that they did all the time. "Tonight will be your last night sleeping alone. After tonight you'll always have one of us around you."

"Umm, are you joking?" I asked.

"No, that's what our pack does," he said. "We are going to get acquainted with you. Before we impregnate you."

"Get me pregnant?!"

"Yes, sweetheart. That's how pack life works," said Jatix. "You're going to carry multiple babies for our pack, and our pack will be powerful."

I took another bite of pasta to avoid replying to that. *How would he feel knowing my fertility could be messed up?* I begged my dad not to make me take so many heat suppressant pills.

"My mother would be happy once we tell her we're in a long-term relationship with an omega," said Silus.

"Have you ever been in a long-term relationship?" I asked curiously.

"Na, we went through females like candy," said Silus.

"What?" I said, blinking. Was I just another one of those *females* to them?

"Yes, Jatix never looked for anything serious," explained Silus. "Commitment issues, that one."

"It's not like that," said Jatix, his eyes flashing at Silus.

"May I be excused?" I said, getting up and carrying my plate. "I'm drained and would love to rest tonight."

"Yes, of course," said Jatix quickly, focusing on Silus. Darius looked equally pissed off. I didn't care how angry they were right now. I was angrier. Throwing away the paper plate, I quickly ascended the stairs. I needed to get away. To think about my situation and figure it out.

Once I was in the room that I was assigned, I didn't dare look at the nest. I didn't want to make myself comfortable at all here.

I dug around the drawers for something to wear and found a small pocket knife in the top drawer. I set it back down and looked in all the drawers for pajamas. I finally found a stack of them folded up. There were just sheer nightgowns and lingerie. I chose a red nightgown with the most coverage in case anyone came in. I made sure there were tags on it first too. I removed my dress, pulling on the soft little gown that went down to my knees. It wasn't the most flattering, but it was better than anything I wore back home.

I turned the lights off and laid in the soft bed. *Gosh, it felt so good.* I stretched flat on my back, closing my eyes and feeling it. I had no idea how long this fantasy life would last for me.

The men had clearly never been serious about anyone before.

What reason did they have to respect me at all? On top of that, Jatix wanted someone to carry babies for him. I had no idea if I was capable of even doing that. As a doctor, I knew taking heat suppressants for a long time could prevent an omega from having babies in the future. Studies were done on omegas who had taken the pills until they were in their forties and had been rendered infertile later in life.

I took more than one a day, which was way more than the required dosage. I was twenty-seven, but that was still dangerous. It would be a dream come true if I ended up having a baby. Well, next to being a doctor, of course. But my happiness didn't matter.

I was just a leftover omega purchased from an auction.

The following day, I rummaged around the room for a pair of pants. But all I saw were dresses. Dresses made me feel open and vulnerable. Giving up, I pulled a black and white dotted summer dress from the hanger. The house was quiet as I tiptoed down the stairs. I didn't want to announce my presence, especially if the pack was still sleeping.

There was no one downstairs. I wondered where they all were. It was pretty early in the day, so that would explain it. They could be sleeping or at work. I spotted a set of keys on the fireplace mantel. They were the keys to Jatix's car. I knew it was his because of the braided lanyard he had attached to them. While he was driving yesterday, I noticed it.

I fantasized about taking the keys and running away. After all, this pack didn't like me. *They had tons of females before. What was I to them?* Maybe Jade and her family could help me out if I left. They could pool together some money and purchase me away from this pack.

I carefully lifted the keys, trying not to make a racket of myself. Walking to the front door of the house, I quietly snapped the locks open and walked out to the front to the sleek sports car of Jatix's.

Razor-focused, I twisted the key into the driver's side and quickly hopped inside. I softly shut the door and placed the key into the ignition.

I nearly screamed when I felt a hand on mine, stopping me. The hand was attached to Silus, sitting there with a smirk on his face.

"What the hell are you doing here?!" I shrieked.

Chapter 14

Silus

It had taken the little omega forever this morning, but she fell into my little trap. I had to test her loyalty to the pack, and it was the only way. Seeing the look of shock on her face made my dick hard.

"The question is. What the hell are *you* doing here?" I countered, clasping her hand tight in mine. She looked so damn juicy in her little dress. My gaze instantly went to her legs outlined by the dress.

"Please don't tell Jatix," she pleaded, looking up at me with her long eyelashes.

I slowly pulled the keys out of her grasp without hurting her. I inhaled her heavy orange scent getting thicker by the minute. This omega was getting aroused. I held the keys in my other hand and pulled the lever on her chair, tilting it back. She tried to open the door, but I held her hand fast in mine.

"You failed the test, little omega," I muttered, hovering over her. "I left the keys out for you."

"What test?" she spat out. I could tell she was livid.

"A test of loyalty," I said. "I knew there was no way an omega from an auction would care about her pack. You were ready to run."

Fuck, she looked so tempting under me.

Her ample breasts were pushed up in her dress after I leaned her chair back. The outline of her breasts made it damn near impossible to think straight. I wanted to stuff my face in the middle. Or ride my dick in the middle of her juicy breasts. We needed to get this introduction ceremony started already. I wanted a good look at her entire body.

Head to toe, belly to pussy. I needed to see all of her. Opened up thoroughly for us.

"I *do* care," she insisted. "It's because you said you've never been in a serious relationship, so I thought none of you would even care about me. I'm just the omega from an auction."

"You're *not* just an omega from an auction," I said. *Did she really think of herself that way?* "We're grateful you're here, and I don't want to see you go."

She smiled at that. It was a small smile, but that was enough for me.

"Are you sure?"

"Of course, I'm sure," I said. "Now, let's go inside and get your punishment over with."

"What punishment?" she gasped.

I quickly jumped out of the car and went around her side, opening the door and waiting for her to step out.

"Come on out," I coaxed.

"I'm not going with you," she said petulantly, looking straight ahead.

"Why not?"

"It's going to hurt," she said, tears streaming down her face.

"What's going to hurt?"

"The punishment."

"It's not that bad," I said. I didn't understand why she was over-reacting. Most omegas enjoyed this part, and I enjoyed it even more. "Just a couple of spanks, that's all."

"I'm not getting out."

"Alright, that's enough," I growled. Bending down, I pulled her out of the car and placed her over my shoulder.

She started kicking and screaming. *Let her kick and scream.* She was a spoiled little brat who needed to get disciplined. The more she clawed at my neck, the hornier I got. When I entered the house, I saw the men drinking coffee with the news on TV.

"What have you got there?" said Jatix, gazing at our omega's bottom hanging in the air as he drank his coffee.

"She tried to escape," I said, waving his keys in his face. "I told you."

I set her down, and we all looked at the tears running down her face.

"Whoa, whoa, why are you crying, my sweet?" said Jatix, forgetting his coffee and rushing to her side.

"Don't hurt me," she begged.

He hugged her tight, looking at me accusingly.

"I would never hurt you," said Jatix. "Why are you thinking that I would?"

"Silus said I would have to get punished," she said, her voice muffled against his white and gold bathrobe.

God, she was doing this on purpose. Trying to act all damn innocent.

"She tried to escape," I growled.

"It's just a couple of spanks, nothing more," said Jatix. "I promise it'll feel good. Lots of omegas find pleasure in it. It's all sexual fun."

"Oh, okay," she said, her gaze curious.

"Now go have some pancakes with Shawn over there. I need to have a word with Silus," said Jatix, patting her butt.

Great, now *I* was going to be the one in the hot seat.

"What?" I said when we were standing outside the house, away from Keera's hearing. Jatix sighed and gazed out at the ocean.

"There is something I neglected to mention to you and Shawn," said Jatix. "After the auction, her father strangled her, and I was late to it. I stopped him eventually, but it showed me that she had gone through some pretty dark times."

"Oh, what the fuck?" I was mind-boggled. *Why hadn't Jatix mentioned it earlier to me?*

"Even I thought she was a hardcore sarcastic doctor," said Jatix. "She still is, but her insecurities are coming out now the longer she stays with us. I can tell she doesn't want to trust fully yet."

"What do we do then?"

"Well, first thing, it's not going to stop me from the introduction ceremony. She'll get used to us," said Jatix confidently. "When she goes into heat, she'll need us inside her."

I wondered when she would eventually go into heat. I felt bad scaring her, and it would be a long while now before she could trust me.

Keera

Shawn made me feel more comfortable after Silus caught me this morning.

I didn't understand why my limbs were trembling. I hadn't had a panic attack in such a long time. Living one day with this pack had made me soft, and I didn't like it. I ate the last bite of the pancake as Shawn was talking about his grandmother.

"I would love to take you there to see her," said Shawn.

"She sounds like a sweetheart," I said, licking off the remaining syrup from my fork. "I would love to visit with you one day."

I heard slippers shuffle behind me, and I looked behind me to see that Jatix was back.

A sliver of worry went through me.

He said that the punishment wasn't going to hurt. Every time I heard the word 'discipline,' it wasn't good. It meant pain to come for days when living with my father. He would grab anything around him, a belt or shoe. It didn't matter to him. As long as I ended up crying, then he was satisfied. Nightmares still plagued me at night. Sometimes I'd be too terrified to fall asleep again. So I'd stay up reading books and being transported to a different world.

"It's time," said Jatix, holding his hand out to me. I gulped, taking his hand. I walked beside him, and the rest of the men trailed behind us. We walked down a set of stairs and down to the basement. Jatix swung open the door with a flourish.

"What is this?" I asked, seeing various contraptions hanging from the ceilings and shelves of colorful devices.

"Welcome to The Naughty Room. This is where you will get your discipline and playtime," said Jatix. "We got rid of the hideous beds in the back."

"They fucking looked like gurneys," Darius pitched in.

My heart raced as I took in the room full of naughty playthings. Upon closer inspection, I was starting to notice the beads and plugs. There was a large sectional where it could sit a group of people as they could watch someone on the swings above. *Are they going to put me on one of those swings?*

"Since you tried to run away," said Jatix. "We have to, unfortunately, punish your bottom. I need you to kneel and grab the stirrups above."

I noticed black handles hanging down from the ceiling. *Jatix promised this wouldn't hurt.*

I knelt on the gold-colored carpeted ground, my knees sinking into the plush carpet. My dress was lifted up over my head, and I grew ashamed as my ass was exposed to them. Jatix pulled my underwear up, causing me to have a wedgie as my panties sunk deep between my butt cheeks and pulled tight on my pussy. The friction against my pussy felt hot, and I wanted more. My body heated as he continued to pull the panties up higher.

Once he was satisfied, I heard a loud snap of one of the feathered whips. I froze. Too scared to breathe.

I shut my eyes tight, scared of the impact. My body trembled when he cracked the whip down on my left cheek. It felt like a human hand, the end of it wide and rubbery.

I cried out when I felt the initial sting. It didn't hurt that bad, but it still stung.

I felt my underwear start getting soaked with my slick automatically with each stroke, and I concentrated on the pleasure of that. He brought the whip down again on my other cheek. It burned for a second, and wetness pooled between my legs. I had never had such a punishment before. The thought of all those men watching me bent over and humiliated excited me like I had never thought before.

"What a beautiful shade of red," said Silus.

"Perfection," said Darius.

"Harder," I moaned, feeling my pussy clench with each compliment.

"That's enough punishment, sweetheart," said Jatix, coming to my side and laying my head down on his lap as he rubbed my ass with a cream. The cream cooled my skin instantly, and my breathing slowed down from the adrenaline. I felt his palm calmly rubbing my skin in circles and his chest rumbled in purrs. "You did such a good job. Did you learn your lesson about running away, little omega?"

"Yes," I whispered.

"Good. Now stand up and take off your dress."

As I stood up, I felt my ass burn with every move. I lifted my dress over my head, conscious that I hadn't worn a bra today. I felt embarrassed standing there with my breasts exposed and panties twisted into a thong.

"What now?" I asked, trying to cover my boobs with my hands.

"We're going to saddle you up in the sex swing," said Jatix, a crazy gleam in his eye. "I'm sure my pack can't wait to see you spread out like a buffet for them."

Before I could think twice about what he said, I yelled out as I was suddenly lifted into the air by Darius and Silus. They strapped me into the swing with both legs up in the air. My ankles were strapped, as well as my wrists.

I was sitting there with my legs spread out and up. The only thing covering me was my panties now, which barely covered my butt hanging out on the edge of the swing. Jatix licked his lips and ran his finger from my toe down to my inner thigh. It was a light touch but powerful at the same time.

I almost orgasmed right there.

His pointer finger lingered on my inner thigh and went further up toward my panties.

Please, I begged in my mind. My inner omega was going crazy. *Please just take it off and fuck me hard. Fuck me until my pussy is full and nice.*

Chapter 15

Jatix

My cock was throbbing. I wanted to go inside her so badly. To put my seed into her. To cause her belly to swell with my child. Tracing her panties, I noticed the dark stain where she wet herself with slick. My Keera was horny, but she was quiet. She was a shy one when it came to sex.

"Men, you can explore now," I said. And immediately, my pack descended on her like wild wolves.

Darius went around behind her, grasping her breasts. The twins stood on either side of her, gently rubbing her thighs.

"Oh my," Keera said, arching her back, wanting me to take her. Her white panties were dark with slick and dripping from the sides, begging to be touched. I pulled her panties to the side, exposing her labia.

"Yes," I whispered, sinfully playing with her slick over her pussy lips. Outlining her pussy with my finger. The room smelled of her. We were completely enveloped in her alluring scent. Her omega magic that called all alphas. A dangerous combination.

I pushed my middle finger inside her and closed my eyes in delight. I pumped her with my finger, going in and out wildly. Her slick squelched around it, more of it spilling out the hornier she became. Darius was licking one breast and squeezing the other. He was a greedy Delta. There was no stopping him.

Shawn was kissing and licking her thighs while Silus sat underneath her, playing with her ass, and tugging on her panties.

Keera

This was like nothing I had ever felt before.

Nothing at all compared to being lusted after by four males. Every part of my skin was being touched, kissed, or licked. My pussy tightened and clenched around Jatix's middle finger, stretching me wide. I was enjoying the Naughty Room a little too much to my surprise

Darius playing with my breasts was the hottest thing I've ever felt. He had claimed one in his greedy mouth, sucking it and causing electric shocks to go through me and straight to my pussy. Silus pulled my underwear down my ass, exposing my butt fully. Every time I tried to concentrate on one touch, my attention was taken to something more shocking.

I felt Silus exploring my bottom, squeezing both cheeks hard.

"Yummy," I heard Silus muttering underneath me when he spread me open.

I clenched hard around Jatix's finger. I couldn't help it as an orgasm ripped through my body, causing my limbs to shake and shudder. I moaned as Jatix pumped faster and faster into my pussy. Silus pressed around my asshole with his fingers and Shawn raked his teeth down my thigh. I screamed as another orgasm took me. Darius licked my hard nipples, and Jatix finally got down and pressed his mouth to my pussy. I felt his tongue rub in circles around my pussy, lapping me up like a hungry wolf.

After my powerful orgasm, my breathing slowed, and I started to feel the burn on my butt from the punishment.

"Time to punish you with my cock," announced Jatix.

Immediately I felt my brain go foggy, and I felt a heavy body press over me. Suffocating me. My eyes rolled back as I began to see black.

"Get her down now!" shouted Darius.

I couldn't hear anything as my ears felt like I had been swimming underwater. *No!* I screamed over and over in my head. I could hear voices, but they were miles away.

Opening my eyes, I saw that I was wrapped in a thin blue blanket and I was lying on someone's lap.

I shot up, seeing Jatix.

"Thank god you're awake," said Jatix. I could hear the relief in his voice.

I saw that we were still in the basement with all the sex swings and toys around us. Everyone was gathered around me. Shawn was sitting directly in front of me on the floor.

"Are you okay?" Shawn asked. "You lost consciousness all of a sudden."

And I knew why. It all hit me. I had buried that memory for so long, and it was bound to emerge one day.

"What happened?" asked Darius.

"I...I had a bad memory," I said. "I didn't think I'd lose it like that. Maybe I need to see a psychiatrist or something."

"What memory?" Jatix pressed, laying his hand on my thigh.

I didn't want to tell them. To admit how broken I felt or the horror I went through. But they had already seen it.

"My dad violated me when I was sixteen," I breathed, pulling the blanket tighter around me. My nails nearly ripped through the fabric. "He did it a couple of times. It's why he wanted me to take so many heat suppressants and pills. He said it was my fault that Mom died, so I had to take her place."

Shocked silence. Not one man breathed a word.

I shut my eyes tight, feeling sick to my stomach. I knew this was too much to tell them. They would never respect me after this.

"He's sick," said Jatix with tight rage in his voice. "How could he do that? No fatherly protective instinct? *What the actual fuck*?!"

Jatix paced around the basement, balling his hands into fists. The room was silent for a few minutes as the men tried to process this information.

"Let's go," said Darius, nodding to Jatix.

"We'll be back," said Jatix to me, kissing me on the forehead before he rushed out of the room with Darius. It all happened in seconds as I sat there, confused about what the hell just happened.

"Are they going after my father?" I asked Silus.

"Most likely," said Silus, his jaw tight as he looked straight ahead. He was also thinking about what I had just revealed to them. "Shawn and I will stay and look after you while they take care of business."

"No, I need to go stop them," I whispered, standing on shaky legs and dropping the blanket. I ran over to my abandoned dress and pulled it on with trembling fingers. It felt like a full five minutes wrestling with the dress. "Please, Silus. I need a ride to my father's house."

"Let them do their job," said Silus quietly, touching my shoulder.

"I think she needs to go see him," said Shawn. "If Jatix goes psycho and kills him, she needs the chance for closure, or she'll hate us all."

"Silus," I said again.

"Fine," he said, resigned at last.

When we pulled up to my old house, I saw Jatix's car parked in the driveway. So he *had* come here to kill him.

My heart pounding, I ran out of Silus's car and towards the open front door, which was wide open. I heard a shout as Silus chased after me in the driveway. Bursting into the house, I saw Darius standing above my dad, his knuckles bloody. My dad was trying to get off the ground, his face covered in blood.

My dad's eyes trained on me when I burst into the living room. He looked like he was in distress. I knew at that moment he wanted help from me. To call my pack off him. But *he* never helped me.

He never helped me when Mom died. He made things worse. He never helped me when he beat me up or violated me. So I simply stood there and watched as Darius punched him again. And again. My lips turned up in a small smile as I watched my father's pain intensify with every kick and punch from Darius and Jatix.

"That's enough," I finally said.

"Are you sure?" Jatix asked as they backed away from his bloody, unconscious body.

"Yes, I don't want you to get locked up for murder," I said.

I walked over to my dad, and I was no longer trembling in his presence. I laid my hand on his chest- his heart still beating.

He had empty beer bottles around him. I was surprised because he usually reserved his drinking at night. His jeans had splatters of cheese sauce from the nachos he had discarded on the small coffee table. I patted his pockets and pulled his wallet out. Opening it, I grabbed my debit card from it. He didn't need that anymore.

"Shit, he takes your money?" exclaimed Jatix. "I would kick the shit out of him again, but that would kill his sorry ass."

"Yes, he did," I said, grabbing the card tightly in my hand. It was probably empty.

Silus gently held my forearm as we walked back to his car. I didn't even realize Shawn had left the backseat to follow us. Silus began to drive away from the house when we all settled into the car. I looked back at my old home, wondering how it all came down to this.

My dad had brought it upon himself.

"How do you feel?" Silus asked.

"Like a weight's been lifted, honestly," I replied. "I didn't think he had that much power over me until I saw him on the ground today. I could do whatever I want now."

"That's amazing," said Shawn. "You *should* be able to do whatever you want."

"Should we listen to some music?" I suggested. I wanted to forget this had happened already. I suddenly felt like a bad daughter since I had sought his approval my whole life. It was my fault Mom died, and now my dad was lying unconscious in his own home. If I thought too hard about it, I would go into a deep depression.

"Fine by me," said Silus, turning on a soundtrack. Loud rock music played, and I rolled down the window, shaking my head wildly. Shawn was also dancing in the back to the beat, the car shaking with our movements. I felt so much freer and lighter than I've ever had.

"Let's do something tonight," said Shawn.

"Ocean?" I suggested.

"Skinny-dipping," said Silus, and I laughed.

"Let's do it," I said, not caring about anything anymore. I would go to all the dances and balls in the world now. I would visit friends anytime. And it was time to find a new job and keep my money to myself.

Chapter 16

Jatix

"What the hell are they doing?" I said out loud.

Keera, Shawn, and Silus were swimming in the ocean, lit by the orange sunset. They were naked and splashing water everywhere. Shawn's belly was jiggling, and Keera's laughter could be heard from afar. She was starting to assimilate well into my pack.

"She's celebrating," said Darius matter-of-factly as he sat in the passenger side, also staring at the wild party on the ocean side. I parked the car up the driveway and could still hear the screaming and shouting below us.

"Good. At least she doesn't hate us," I said, relieved.

"But next time, we need to control our impulses more. Keera has every right to run away from us."

"Hell no," I said. "Her father committed a crime and should be locked up. I'll talk to her tonight if she wants to do that and go through with bringing him to justice."

"She has to," said Darius.

"Let's go frolic in the water with them," I said, knowing damn well

Darius would never do that.

As I walked to meet them, I couldn't help but stare at our omega in admiration. She was stronger than I thought she was. Water dripped off her hard pink nipples as the water receded, showing off her nude body.

Fuck, not again.

My cock had a mind of its own as it hardened.

I watched intently as she turned to Shawn, bending down to splash water on him. Her naked bottom fully on display. Her luscious black hair stopped at the curve of her ass, wildly swinging around her breasts.

The closer I got, the more I felt my blood rush to my penis. My heart pounded hard as I approached. I needed to bring up having babies and if she was willing to. I didn't want to scare her, but it was imperative to me to know what she thought of it. I needed someone who was serious. I was fucking forty-four years old.

And I wanted it with her.

"You're here!" exclaimed Keera, hugging me with wild abandon, soaking me in the salty ocean water. Her skin smelled like the ocean mixed with her natural omega scent.

"I'm here," I said dryly, looking down at my wet robes.

"Oops, sorry," she said, anxiously wringing her hands. "I just wanted to thank you so much for what you did. I didn't think it would feel this good, but it helped me so much."

"No problem, kitten," I said, bringing my hand around her neck and pulling her towards me. I planted a kiss right on her lips, and she blinked in surprise. I pressed my lips more firmly over hers, and her eyelashes fluttered as she closed her eyes. The kiss was all out consuming my emotions as I pulled her closer, and her waist naturally arched towards mine, right on top of my hard cock.

She pulled away, licking her lips. Her pink tongue teasing me.

"Strip," she said. "Let's play in the water first, then later..."

She winked. And I swore my balls tightened in anticipation for tonight.

Suddenly a huge splash of water swept over my head, soaking my entire robe. I turned to my left, and Silus stood there with an evil smirk on his face.

"Fuck you, Silus!" I shouted, ripping off my robe. These guys were just jealous. They could've fucking kissed her instead of playing like babies in the water. I chased him into the water, the cold water instantly hitting my legs, my hard cock swinging in front of me. Silus fled deeper into the water as I ran after him. "You're such a fucking baby, Silus."

I could hear Shawn and Keera laughing behind me as I raged at the cockblocker.

Keera

That night, I sat exhausted in the dining room.

Darius had ordered pizza for dinner while we played in the ocean, and it smelled divine. My arms felt like lead, and my legs hurt. After all the fun in the water, I took a shower with Jatix. And things had taken a wild turn in the shower with him. I knew he was horny, and I wanted to please him, so another blowjob in the shower did the trick for him. I wore a silky pair of red pajamas with a cozy cotton red robe after being in the freezing water for hours.

"I ordered a cheese, a veggie, and a pepperoni pizza," said Darius. He was sitting next to me, and I leaned my head against his upper arm in my tiredness. It had been a very long day for me. With supercharged emotions and feelings of guilt at the same time. "I wasn't sure which one you liked."

"Veggie is my favorite," I said, breathing in the aroma as Jatix quickly opened the box at my words. Grabbing a couple of slices, I dropped the extra hot slices onto my plate.

"Same," said Silus, also grabbing the veggie slices. I couldn't help but admire his biceps as he reached across the table. "Pizza, in general, is the worst on my body. Lately, we haven't been eating healthy since you arrived, Keera. Life has been upside down."

"Sorry," I said, blowing on the hot slice. "I could tell you work hard on your body."

"Don't ever be sorry," said Shawn quickly. "Silus is being stupid. He can make his own damn food, but he's lazy. What are your favorite foods?"

I was touched by how quickly Shawn answered. But I also had a creepy feeling that Shawn enjoyed watching me eat.

"Anything with cheese on it," I said, and Silus groaned. "Whoops."

"And that's what I'll make," said Shawn, biting into his cheesy slice of pizza.

"Glad I ordered pizza then," said Darius digging in. The pizza tasted delicious as I took bite after bite. Food was the best after being in the water all day. Jatix's purple eyes were focused on me, and I gulped. He had something on his mind.

"Keera, do you remember our conversation about babies?" Jatix finally asked.

My heart sank.

"Yes," I said. I couldn't forget that. They had bought me, and I was theirs to do as they pleased.

"When do you go into heat next? Do you feel it coming soon?"

"I don't know," I said, my gaze on the second slice of pizza and the juicy cheese sliding off the crust. *Should I tell him the truth? Would he cast me out forever?*

"What do you mean?" he asked. "You can tell me anything, Keera."

"So when I lived with my dad, he made me take multiple heat suppressant pills..."

"Okay?"

"It can cause infertility," I said finally. I looked up at him, and his face didn't show any emotion. But I could see him thinking. "It means I may never go into heat. Like ever."

I watched as Jatix closed his eyes in frustration. He rubbed the back of his neck. Then he opened his eyes again.

"I'm sorry for what your father made you go through," he said. "He ruined your future and your life."

"I know you want babies," I said. Then I contemplated a horrible thought. *What if Jatix took a second omega?* It was rare because omegas were territorial, but in an extreme case like this, it was necessary. I almost wanted to cry.

The table was quiet at my revelation, and I had to get out there.

Upstairs in my room, I huddled in my nest.

I needed some comfort. It had been a tense morning at my dad's house, but it ended up with me being closer to the Lustfur Pack than ever before, and now I was scared to lose them to a new omega.

Shawn was so sweet to me in every way. Darius was the type to defend me from anything, and Silus made me laugh a lot. Jatix turned me on like no other alpha. He was wild and open with sex which I loved. He made me feel more comfortable and less shy about everything.

I grabbed a book from the pile and saw it was a romance book about vampires. I scoffed. We never got along with vampires, and I couldn't imagine ever meeting one. They had hunted omegas and betas for years until the Alphas, Deltas, and Sigmas got together and pushed them off our island. I had no idea where the vampires resided now; there were always rumors that they were still living amongst us but in hiding.

The book was a romance between an omega and a vampire. *Eww, why the hell does Jatix have this here?*

I picked up another book. This time it looked more promising. It was a hot devil romance with a picture of a muscular Lucifer on the front. *Much better.*

I settled in my blankets and began reading. I was around too much masculine energy today, and it felt nice to listen to the heroine. As I turned page twenty, I heard a knock at the door. *Noo*, I was just getting to the sexy part of the book.

"Come in," I called.

I could see the men walk into my room as I watched behind the sheer curtains of my nest. They pulled the curtain aside, and they all settled around me. *What did they want? Was Jatix going to tell me they were taking on another omega?*

Jatix laid next to me and gently pulled the book from my hands, setting it down in the pile of books in the corner. Silus lay on my other side, with Darius sitting cross-legged in front of me and Shawn laid at my feet.

"First off," said Jatix, rubbing my arms under the blanket. He looked at me intently, and I felt my stomach clench when he looked at me like that. "I'm not letting you go anywhere."

"Are you going to take a second omega?" I asked.

"Never," said Jatix. "I accept you even if you can't go into heat. But I will try my best to bring you to heat."

"That's impossible," I said.

"We're going to do it the old-fashioned way."

"And what is that?" I asked, a little scared. I had never heard of an old-fashioned way. But after all, he was twenty-plus years older than me.

"We're going to use our alpha pheromones on you. We will rub up against you all night," said Jatix. "Your omega instincts will kick in, knowing an alpha is ready to go into rut when you go into heat. We will rut you as soon as your heat comes in."

"And you really think this will work?" I asked.

I had never heard of this technique before, but I wouldn't mind all the cuddling that was going to happen. And who knows, maybe we'll have sex too. I've been unimaginably teased over the past couple of days, and I needed some sort of relief.

"It should work. But you have to remain calm and not stressed," said Jatix, holding my hand in his. "Even if it doesn't happen right away, I will wait patiently for you. Even if it takes our lifetime."

"But what if it doesn't work?"

"Then you're still mine."

Chapter 17

Keera

I smiled. Relief flowed through me when he said that. I didn't know whether it would be a good thing or a bad thing, but I hoped he meant what he said and wasn't lying. But his gaze conveyed honesty, and I couldn't help but melt when he looked at me like that. Like he couldn't bear to lose me.

"Let's go to the bed," suggested Darius, excitement twinkling in his eyes. My heart started to beat faster with excitement too. It would be my first time being surrounded by multiple males in the same bed.

"I guess we'll need more space. It's a bit cramped in here," I said, looking at everyone squished into my little nest with me. It felt cozy, but it wasn't ideal for what we were going to try. Darius grasped my hand, helping me up, and I realized just how massive he was standing in front of me. He was all muscle. He winked when he noticed me checking him out, and I blushed, looking away.

Heading to the bed, we piled into it, with me in the middle.

I laid on my back, and Jatix lowered himself on top of me. His knees were on either side of me. His peppermint scent enveloped me as he held me tight against him. I inhaled his scent deeply, closing my eyes as he rubbed his face against my face, cheek against cheek. Shawn and Silus closed in on me on both sides. Alpha energy surrounded me. I felt my inner omega stirring and my core clenching with need and arousal.

"God, you feel so fucking good under me," Jatix purred in my ear. "My alpha needs your omega to submit. To go into heat."

Slick drenched my underwear as he rubbed his whole body against me. I could feel every tendon and every muscle as he rested most of his body weight on me. I wrapped my hands around his back, twisting my fingers together as I breathed in his scent.

"Oh," I whispered, humping upwards when I felt his cock press against my pussy.

"My alpha cock is hard for you," he muttered in my ear, and my face heated. "Why are you blushing, sweetheart?"

"Your dirty talk," I said.

"So pure, so innocent," he said, rubbing my thighs. My heart lifted, and for some reason, I didn't feel as damaged and dirty after remembering what my father did to me. Jatix's presence and care affected me in ways he would never know or understand. "Let's take off your clothes, sweetheart. I need to feel your naked body squirming underneath me."

He sat up and pulled his clothes off, his eyes never leaving me. I bit my lip and pulled my dress over my head with Silus's help. His brother, Shawn, unsnapped my bra and tossed it to the ground. When we were both naked, Jatix laid on top of me again, and I welcomed the nearness of his body against mine.

Skin to skin. His alpha body heat against mine. We lay like that for a few minutes, then he brought his lips to mine, kissing me. His hair framed my face, enclosing us in our togetherness. It was just him and I alone in our bubble as we kissed.

Something inside me was stirring, causing something foreign inside me to wake up. Tendrils of warmth started at my pussy, but did not go all the way up to my belly. The warmth and heat wouldn't go all the way to my womb. I wrapped my hands around Jatix's neck, kissing him harder as he rubbed up on me. His lips were locked onto mine as our kiss deepened.

I felt his hard erection against my pussy. A reminder of an alpha who needed his omega.

"I keep feeling the warmth in my pussy, but it just stops there," I said.

"It's okay. We're going to keep trying every day. Until you feel the heat in your belly," said Jatix, kissing my neck. His cock against my pussy teased me like nothing else. I wanted him to go inside me and stretch me with his cock and eventually his knot. I was desperate to know how it felt when I actually wanted it. I never felt like this before in my entire life.

"I need you," I whispered.

"Not yet little omega," said Jatix. "We need to trigger your highest state of arousal. Silus take over."

Silus took Jatix's place on top of me, and I touched his heavily tattooed arms as he leaned his naked body against mine. His muscles flexed as he rubbed against my skin, going up and down. He pressed his lips to mine, to my surprise. His lips were firm and lean. Sexual hunger fully present in his hard kiss.

Silus pressed his tongue into my mouth, and it soon turned out of control. Our tongues wrestled, and my pussy throbbed with need. His heavy cock pressed against my thighs, ready to enter me. I spread my legs wider and arched myself towards him as I inhaled his musky alpha scent.

"Oh yes, baby, arch your hips like that," he said, pressing his thumb against my clit in circles. "Aren't you a sexy kitten?"

I let out a purr of satisfaction as he showed me his alpha dominance. The need for a cock to plunge deep into my slick-ridden pussy was getting stronger. I wondered how long this might last and it was harder than I thought it would be.

"Do you want me Silus?" I asked.

"More than you can ever imagine," he grunted, kissing me again on the lips.

"My turn," said Shawn.

Silus groaned and rolled off me, squeezing my left breast as Shawn hovered over me already completely naked. I gazed into his eyes and his long dark eyelashes. His gaze captured mine and my body temperature was starting to heat up again.

"I know this is weird, but will you allow me to rub myself all over you?" Shawn asked.

"I guess," I giggled through my arousal. "I need your alpha pheromones."

He lifted his body, so his full weight didn't crush me when he lowered himself onto me. His belly pressed against my pussy, arousing me even more as he against me rubbed up and down.

"Can I kiss you?" he whispered.

"Just kiss her, goddamn it," muttered Jatix as he rubbed my thigh.

Silus was kissing my hair. They were all purposely breathing on me, marking me with their scent. If another alpha came my way, they would know I was clearly taken.

I loved the feeling of Shawn's lips against mine. We kissed for a few minutes as he humped against me, causing my pussy to go haywire. I wrapped my legs around his waist, trying to pull him closer to me. His cock pressed on the outside of my vagina, nearly going inside me.

"I'm going to go inside you," he said, looking at me intensely. His gray eyes gazed into mine.

"Yes," I moaned.

"Nope, that's enough," growled Jatix, pushing Shawn off me. I looked at Jatix in surprise. Shawn's face turned red. "We have to make her needy for us, and that will get her heat to happen. No orgasm or release for her."

"No," I whined, grabbing Jatix's hard cock and stroking it up and down as he sat over me.

"You better stop it, sweetheart. Unless you want to be punished," he said. "We are all going to sleep around you now."

"Wait, where's Darius?" I asked, sitting up.

"He said he's not an alpha and didn't want to ruin it," said Silus.

"It doesn't matter. Isn't he part of this pack?" I demanded, climbing over the alphas' huge bodies.

I found Darius pacing up and down the hallway.

"What are you doing out here?" he asked when he saw me standing there. His eyes nearly bugged out when he noticed that I was completely naked.

"Looking for you," I said.

"I'm not an alpha," he said. "It might mess up the process."

"I want you with me," I said, walking over to him and grabbing his reluctant hands. "I would rather mess up the process than not have you in there with me."

He looked at me with unbelievingly.

"You've got to be joking," he said. "The most important thing to an omega is going in heat and getting rutted by an alpha."

"I don't care about all that," I said, meaning it. The little time I spent with Darius, the more I wanted to be with him. I wanted him with me, without question.

"You getting stressed isn't helping," he finally relented, his gaze lowering to my boobs and my navel. I could feel the slick between my legs, and I clenched my thighs tight. "Don't fight the slick."

He pressed his hand between my thighs, separating them. I gladly spread my legs for him, desperate for release. Then he rubbed his fingers over my pussy, and I moaned at his touch. He was so masculine, and the dominance turned me on more than anything.

"Will you come to bed with me?" I breathed. Focused on his finger inserted inside me.

"Yes," he said huskily.

We walked hand in hand towards the bedroom.

"Decided to come to your senses?" Jatix asked Darius.

"Now there's no way I'm missing out," said Darius, quickly unbuckling his belt and ripping off his clothes. I blushed and smiled as I crossed the room to the bed between Shawn and Silus. Before I knew it, Darius's muscular body was on top of mine. My breathing quickened with arousal as I took in his golden skin and tattooed body. The earring on his ear shone from the moonlight in the room.

"I missed you when you didn't join us at the ocean," I said in a quiet voice. He looked instantly regretful.

"Next time," he said, lowering his mouth to my collarbone and pressing soft kisses all around. My skin heated when he did that. "I'll make it up to you, baby."

"You better," I said, running my finger down his hairy chest.

"*Fuck.* When you do that..." said Darius, and I felt his cock press against me as he hugged me to him. The others were touching various parts of my body until I lost track of who was touching me. We cuddled, and he hugged me to him for several minutes, with the passion growing between us. It was becoming more intense, and I craved release.

"Please touch me," I begged.

"No," said Jatix sharply. "This is a good thing, omega, I promise. Darius, let me take over before you fuck her senseless. You look close to jackhammering into her pussy."

"Fuck yes, I'm close to sticking my cock into her," growled Darius, unwilling to move from on top of me. He groaned when he finally complied and moved over for Jatix. "I'll turn on the fan, it's getting hot as fuck in here."

All night long, the males' bodies were pressed to mine, driving me nuts until I yawned from exhaustion.

"Sleep tight, sweetie," said Jatix, kissing my shoulder as he laid beside me.

The next morning, Jatix kissed me on the lips, muttering about going to work. I mumbled and turned to my other side. I didn't even hear the door as I went back to sleep. I opened my eyes after sleeping for another twenty minutes. I realized I was alone in the bed.

Stretching, I wondered where they had all disappeared to. I smiled, remembering last night. I placed my hand over my belly, remembering how turned on I was before I fell asleep, cocooned between Darius and Jatix. It was the best night of my life. I felt extra secure in Darius's arms and I slept like a baby.

Getting out of bed was painful.

My muscles were sore from the pack's intense urgency to have me go into heat. My legs were sore from clenching around each guy's waist. I haven't gone into heat yet and began doubting the methods Jatix was using. I wondered if it was for real or if I would go into heat right away. If not, I would be fine, but I always dreamt of starting a family of my own. Holding my future baby in my arms would be the ultimate feeling of contentment. I would never think of my father again after that.

I brushed and took a quick shower before any alpha saw and joined me. When one of them knew I was taking a shower, it was inevitable that they would join me. I needed time alone this morning. Wrapped in a towel, I rummaged through the clothes in the closet for something to wear. I looked up at the shelves and hadn't noticed a pile of folded clothes on the top. I pulled it down, seeing they were leggings, tank tops, and shirts. I pulled on leopard print leggings and a black tank top. I was relieved to have something normal to wear.

I needed to go shopping for my own style of clothes and thought about finding a job soon. I was too shy to ask Jatix, even though they *were* supposed to take care of their omega. I looked out the window, which had a direct view of the backyard.

I noticed Darius and Silus were working out, and my heart swelled with excitement upon seeing them. It was a Monday, and I knew Shawn mentioned he had work, so he was probably gone. My gaze rested on Darius's bare chest, which was sweaty and gleaming from his workout. When he began to do pushups, I couldn't help but look at his toned ass clenching. My pussy throbbed the longer I stared at them. Silus was lifting himself on the bars, and my pussy tingled to life, watching the sweat bead off his arms. His ear piercing shined in the sun.

I decided I needed some exercise too.

Chapter 18

Darius

"Last night was amazing," said Silus, lifting weights next to me. "I wish Jatix would let us have our way with her."

I set the weights down for a breather.

"Fuckin agreed," I said. "She wants us too."

"I wonder if Keera is awake yet."

I was starting to get worried about her. None of us wanted to wake her since she was so sleepy after last night's cuddling session. But it was noon now, and I was getting antsy without her. All our cock energy must have worn her out. I was about to go inside and check on her; until I saw her standing on the other side of the glass door. She tapped on the glass and smiled, coming into the backyard.

Her smile was like an angel. She walked towards us, and I rushed over to her, lifting her in a hug. She squealed as I put her back down.

I kissed her heartily on the lips, and her eyes fluttered closed as she kissed me back.

"You're happy today," she observed, shading her eyes with her hand. She looked so beautiful in her leopard print leggings. Her ass would jiggle with every move, showing off her curves. Her cleavage was ready to spill out in the thin tank top she was wearing. I imagined pressing my face between her bouncy ass cheeks.

Slow down, Darius.

"Good morning, sleepyhead," said Silus, kissing her on the lips as well.

"I want to exercise, too," she announced.

What?

She spotted the large exercise ball and started leaning against it. Her ass faced us as she bounced up and down. I looked at Silus, and Silus's lips twitched. We were both thinking the same thing. This omega was a horny kitten. My dick hardened as I watched her bounce on the pink ball.

"Oh really?" I asked, walking over to her. "You want to join the big bad boys?"

"What do I do on this ball?" she asked slyly, looking at me with hooded eyes.

She thought she was smart, but I knew what she was doing. She was trying to get us to fuck her, and that was against Jatix's orders. I helped straighten her right leg, my hand under her knee.

"Straighten your other leg," I said.

"I can help," said Silus eagerly. He put his hand under her knee. Her bottom jiggled in the middle of us. "Now move forward and back." Her orange scent hit my nose right away with her butt in front of me. This was quite the temptation.

"Oh, this is real exercise," she whined. "I'm getting tired."

"Of course, this is real exercise," I chuckled.

"Keep going. Flex those butt cheeks, baby," said Silus, voice husky. Her butt looked so tempting as she moved up and down, flexing her legs. I couldn't help but smack her on the ass.

"Hey!" she squealed as I grabbed her butt cheek. Silus grabbed her other cheek.

She felt like soft dough in my hand as I kneaded her bottom under my rough palm. I loved the feeling of it. I could smell her scent thickening in the air. She was aroused again, just like last night. I missed that. Last night, I enjoyed smelling her for hours. My dreams were also pleasant for once. "Mhm."

"Why are you teasing us?" asked Silus.

"Maybe because I want you to take me," she whispered. Silus tugged the waistband of her leggings down, exposing her ass while she leaned over the ball. She wore a tiny thong which did nothing to cover her. My dick hardened at the sight.

"Let's go to the guesthouse," I suggested.

"Jatix is gonna kill us if we give her our cocks too early," said Silus, looking around as if Jatix would pop out of nowhere.

"You won't tell anyone, right kitten?" I asked her, my heart pounding with arousal. All the blood flow left my brain and went straight to my dick.

"No," she breathed, her eyes wide as she sat on the ball.

"Do you want us both inside you?"

"Yes," she said eagerly.

There was no way in fuck I was going to refuse her my cock. If she needed it, she was going to have it. She was going to have *all* of me.

118

Mind. Body. Spirit.

Keera

I wasn't prepared for what would happen when I got into the little guest house with an alpha and a delta.

I brushed off any spiders on the bed while Silus blasted the air conditioner. My pussy clenched with every step I made, eager for them to plunge inside me. I had literally been dreaming of this. Finally, Darius came around the bed to where I was.

"Enough cleaning," he said, wrapping his arms around me and kissing my neck. His breath raised the little hairs on my neck. He bent me over on the bed and rubbed my butt with his broad hand. Silus came around the bed, standing in front of me and sandwiching me between them.

Darius pulled my leggings down, and I quickly stepped out of them. I could feel my slick covering my twitching pussy entirely. I was horny as hell. Silus rubbed my pussy over my underwear, and I quickly shimmied off the underwear as well.

"Oh, you want to get down to business already?" said Silus, one eyebrow raised.

"You guys have been teasing me all night," I said, annoyed, throwing my thong to the side.

"You're making me fucking horny," said Silus ripping off his sweatpants. I could already see Darius's grey sweatpants discarded on the floor. Silus lifted me up, and I wrapped my legs around his waist, smelling his alpha sweat. The smell was like nothing I'd ever smelled before. It made my hormones go wild for him. Darius grabbed ahold of my ass cheeks, spreading them wide.

My heart raced. I never put anything in my butt before.

I was scared, but Silus started rubbing my clit with his thumb, and arousal strummed through my body. Taking me to new heights. His touch was distracting me from what was going on back there. Darius spat into my ass, rubbing the moisture around my tiny hole, slowly getting me used to being touched there. This was going to be a hot quickie with the two of them. When his finger slipped inside my tight hole, I cried out when it stung at first.

"Open for me. Don't clench," said Darius, kissing my naked shoulder.

"I can't. I've never done that before," I said.

"Yes, you can. Focus on Silus's finger on your pussy."

I focused on the feelings Silus was arousing in my pussy. He rubbed my clit in circles while Darius rubbed my anus. They were moving in sync somehow. My nerve endings were on fire, both holes ready to be filled.

"I want to fuck your tight pussy," Silus growled.

Silus then speared me with his dick. Ever so slowly, he set me on top of him, lowering me onto his dick more and more until the fullness of it settled inside me. I gasped when the full length was finally inside. While he did that, I didn't realize when Darius pressed a second finger into my asshole, stretching me out a little further. Then Darius removed his fingers, and I gasped when he rubbed his penis against me instead.

"Darius," I said in a panic.

"You're an omega. Your body was made for this," said Darius roughly. He spread my butt cheeks further apart, and I felt him slowly pushing his cock inside my anus. I gasped but my body was quick to adjust to the intrusion. Slowly, inch by inch, stretching my tight hole until he was fully inside me.

He settled there without moving at first.

"You okay, baby?" Silus asked, brushing my hair away from my eyes in concern.

"Yes, let's do it," I whispered.

I was filled in both holes with dick. And it felt amazing.

I held Silus's arm for balance as Darius lifted me by the waist. As he lifted me up and down, both cocks pressed inside me, looking for release. My pussy and asshole clenched around both dicks greedily. I closed my eyes in rapture. The fullness of both dicks inside me was satisfying and something I had been looking forward to as a grown omega longing for a pack of her own.

It was one of my fantasies that I kept deep down.

"You're doing so good," said Silus. "Baby, look at me."

I looked at him and focused on his clear gray eyes as he thrust into me. I moaned as he pushed deeper into me. Darius followed suit. Both hard cocks moving in the same rhythm felt amazing. My core clenched with warmth as an orgasm wracked through me. I was shaking as Silus and Darius held me over their cocks, pounding harder and faster. Faster and faster until they both exploded at the same time inside me.

"Fuck," said Darius, and I felt his hot liquid shoot into me from behind. His penis slowly retracted. Silus's cock stayed inside me and swelled rapidly at the base, holding me tight. Silus pulled me over him on the bed, and I collapsed on top of him, my heart pounding.

This was my first knot. At least, in my mind, it was. I refused to dwell on the horrors of my past. Silus rubbed my back, and I could feel his heartbeat race underneath my ear. His tattoo of a large wolf on his chest intimidated me before, but now all I felt was safety in his arms.

Darius lay next to us, playing with my hair while I was trapped in place by Silus's cock as he knotted me.

"You feel so amazing on top of my cock," said Silus. "I never want this to end."

"I don't either," I said. "This was the sexiest thing ever."

Darius chuckled, his hands behind his head. His spiky blond hair was all mussed up from our sexual romp.

"Imagine doing this every Monday with us," said Darius.

"Don't you both have jobs too?" I asked curiously.

"I do odd jobs here and there," said Darius. "I do guard duty most of the time."

"How about you, Silus?"

"Currently unemployed. Perks of living with a pack," said Silus.

"What?!" I exclaimed.

"I'm kidding," said Silus, flexing his arms. "I'm a personal trainer. I can train your sexy ass anytime."

"I used to be a doctor," I said.

"What happened?" asked Darius.

"I got fired," I said.

"Just go back to the hospital with Jatix and demand your job back," said Silus, and my heart suddenly lifted in hope.

"Really?"

"I say, go for it," said Silus. "Jatix is respected since his father had ties to the Royal Pack. They'll listen."

Silus's knot began to go down, and I rolled off him, laying between them, feeling the air conditioner hit my sweaty skin. It was a hot day today.

"Shall we shower?" said Darius, reading my mind. He seemed to be in tune with every emotion of mine. It was crazy.

"Yeah it looks like there's a bathroom and a shower, too," I said, sitting up. This room had a cozy vibe with its various plants around the corners of the window, the sheer white curtain flew in the breeze, and the tiny television atop the wooden dresser in front of us was rustic and made my heart feel at ease. This would be my new hangout spot if I ever needed to relax.

"Man, Jatix is gonna kill us," said Silus.

"We couldn't help it. She was waving her butt everywhere," said Darius.

"Hey!" I said indignantly. It was true, though. I was horny as fuck and needed them badly. "Unless any of you open your mouths, nothing will happen."

In the shower, it was steamy and it was warm. And I had both Darius and Silus with me in the bathtub. It was much smaller than the master bathroom I had in my room, but we managed to fit.

Darius rubbed his hands all over my front, squeezing my boobs. Silus was behind me, washing my back. They passed a single white bar of soap between each other as they washed me down. In a way, I felt pampered having these men wash me, but it also made me very horny again.

"Your perky tits are nice and shiny. I want to suck on them," said Darius.

My breasts felt heavy with arousal, and I arched my chest out for him to suck on them. His large tongue swirled around my right nipple while he grasped my other boob. Slick shot out from my vagina the faster he swirled his tongue. Silus massaged my bottom with his soapy hands. I never felt so horny so fast.

"You both are turning me on all over again," I said.

"That's the goal, baby," said Silus. "Relax and let us do our jobs to bring you to heat. And maybe Jatix won't freak out that we gave you satisfaction too early."

I let out a tortured moan as Darius stopped licking and began sucking on my boob. Silus knelt in the shower and swirled his tongue around my clit. My pussy throbbed and burned with a need for release. A crescendo of waves roared within me, and my belly clenched tight the hornier I became. Then I felt Silus's finger press into my pussy while he licked my clit. I gripped Darius's arms for balance as I shook.

I screamed as I finally came into his mouth.

"Good girl," said Silus, licking my pussy in slow strokes until I stopped shaking.

Chapter 19

Keera

"You're hiding something," Jatix accused.

I looked away from the movie I was watching with Shawn and Silus. Darius was out changing the tire for his car. I knew it was just an excuse for him to avoid watching the girly movie with us.

"What do you mean?" I asked. I could feel Silus fidgeting next to me as he adjusted himself on the couch, laying his hand on my lap. He squeezed my thigh.

"Silus, what happened?" Jatix interrogated him next. I was wondering how the hell Jatix was suspecting anything. We had remained coy and silent the whole time when Jatix came home.

"What makes you think I'm hiding something?" I asked again, squirming in my seat. "Can't we just watch the movie in peace?"

"Something about your scent," said Jatix, sniffing my neck.

"Fine Jatix," huffed Silus. "We had sex with her. Darius and I."

Shawn gasped audibly, and Jatix rose from the couch. I flinched, seeing his eyes flash.

"You messed up all the progress we made last night," said Jatix, massaging his temple in frustration. "We need to take drastic measures to induce her heat. Keera, be prepared. Also, Silus and Darius will be the last ones to touch you."

"Did you tell him, Silus?" asked Darius, walking into the house.

"Both of you messed up big time," said Jatix.

"I teased them. It was my fault," I said, my heart pounding. I suddenly realized how seriously Jatix was taking this, and I felt bad.

"No, Keera," groaned Silus.

"You will be punished too, Keera," said Jatix. "You will be hand-cuffed to your bed until we bring you to heat."

He was true to his word. Before I knew it, Jatix had thrown me over his shoulder, carrying me up the stairs.

"I'm sorry, Jatix," I said, struggling to get off him. He placed his palm over my butt to hold me still.

"You deliberately disobeyed me, sweetheart," he said gruffly, throwing me onto my bed. "Did you grab the handcuffs from the basement?"

"Yes," said Shawn, and I heard the clink of metal as he passed it to Jatix.

Shawn?!

Why would Shawn help Jatix with this devious plan? I tried to get off the bed, but Shawn held me down, his arm across my middle. He removed my shirt with his other hand, throwing it to the floor.

When Jatix placed the purple furry handcuffs on my wrists, securing me to the bedposts, I was starting to get horny. I was still wearing leggings, underwear, and my bra. Jatix unclasped my bra, releasing my breasts while Shawn pulled my leggings and underwear off.

Jatix snatched the underwear from Shawn. He held it up for all the men to see.

Then he straightened it, displaying the dark wet patch on the seat of my pink panties.

"Her undies are wet," said Jatix. "But it would have been drenched completely if none of you knuckleheads had sex with her. It would have been dripping in slick if you hadn't messed this up."

"Sorry, boss," said Darius.

"Sorry isn't going to cut it," said Jatix, fingering the panties between his thumb and forefinger. I was getting aroused just watching him. "You and Silus will sit to the side and watch. No touching at all."

"What the fuck?" Silus burst out. "*The whole time*?!"

"You will be the very last to touch her," said Jatix. "Shawn will be first since he loves to eat. Shawn, go ahead and start eating her out. Do NOT let her cum."

I wasn't allowed to orgasm?! What the heck rule was that? I've never heard of bringing someone to heat by force, but what did I know after going to medical school.

"I can smell your excitement," said Shawn, gently massaging my closed thighs. "Why won't you open up for me? I want to lick your damp pussy. I'm hungry."

His hair hung low over his eyes, but I could see the passion and intensity behind his gaze. He wanted me, just like any other alpha in the room. He was right about me being excited. Even though I was a little scared, my pussy ached to be touched. Jatix was grasping my breasts and kissing my neck, his favorite area.

I allowed my thighs to fall open, and Shawn used his knees to separate my legs apart. Anticipation strummed through my body. I couldn't wait for Shawn's tongue to touch my clit if it was going to be like the experience I had in the shower with Silus. I craved it again.

Then he laid on his belly, preparing to eat me out.

Shawn

"Looks delicious," I panted.

The sight of her little pink pussy in front of me looked glorious as I lay on my stomach, and I couldn't wait to open her pussy lips and dig in. I pushed her thighs further apart, opening her up a little bit more for me. Her pussy lips glistened under the lights as I spread her legs.

It looked like she was just as eager. Her pink hole was wet with her clear slick. I began by kissing her thighs and slowly made my way up to her center. Her entire pussy was now covered in a sheen of slick. She smelled of strong citrus when she was horny. Like a beautiful open mandarine right in front of me.

I wanted to suck her dry. I was hungry. I pressed my mouth against her pussy, kissing it.

"He's kissing her pussy," I heard Darius mutter. Silus growled.

They're jealous.

I pulled her pussy into my mouth like a suction as I sucked every drop of her slick. She moaned, and her thighs pressed hard on both sides of my head. Keera hadn't spent much time with me, but I was going to make sure I treated her pussy just right. Jatix trusted me with this important job.

She was never going to forget this.

Releasing her pussy from my mouth, I stared at her swollen pink clit. Swiping it with my tongue, I watched as she clenched her pussy, retracting her clit slightly. Pleased that I was having an effect, I circled her clit with my tongue, drawing it out a little more.

"Oh, Shawn," she said desperately.

I stopped. She was close to climaxing already.

"I'm sorry," I said, and she groaned, shaking her handcuffs in frustration. The metal sounds rang in the room. I hated leaving her like this. "I swear I'll give you the best orgasm when you go into heat. I promise."

"Please, Shawn!" she begged, opening her legs wider. "Untie me."

"Nope, little kitten," said Jatix. "No touching yourself, either. Five-minute break, then I'll go next."

Jatix

This was necessary. This was the old-method way to bring an omega to heat by force. I knew Silus and Darius were suffering as they watched, standing around the bed. If my pack disobeyed, they needed to learn a lesson or they'd keep doing this, jeopardizing our chances of having a baby with the omega I loved.

Keera had closed her legs in defiance. She was clearly angry at me.

"Open up, Keera," I ordered.

"No," she said. "If you're just going to tease me, then it's not going to happen."

"Keera," I said again, using the alpha tone to get her to obey. Her breasts heaved up and down in arousal as she quietly spread her legs.

"Please make me cum," she said. "I can't stand it."

I ignored her as I knelt between her legs, holding her thick creamy thighs apart. She was *our* omega, and she was going to have to start obeying me. I've been taking it way too easy on her this whole time, falling under the spell of her pretty eyes.

"Shawn, hand me the anal plug," I said. "The vibrator too."

"What?" she gasped out, trying to close her legs, but I kept them open, gripping her thighs to hold her still.

"Oh shit, psycho Jatix is back," said Silus.

I took the anal plug from Shawn. The metal drop felt cool in my hand. The end was studded in red rubies.

"Lift her legs up," I ordered, and Shawn hastily obeyed.

Keera's handcuffs were going crazy as the metal clanged against the bedposts. As she struggled against Shawn's grip, I watched her little bottom squirming on the bed, trying to get away from the plug. I rubbed the plug against her wet pussy, lubing it up with her slick. Her bottom rocked back and forth. The sight of her butt wiggling made my cock hard. It was time to stick it in her. I needed to see the plug inside her ass.

I then spread her ass cheeks apart, displaying her dark, puckered hole.

"Hold still, or else it could hurt," warned Shawn, and Keera finally stopped squirming.

I ran my thumb around her little hole, feeling the tiny bumps and ridges. She was clenching tight, her anus refusing to relax. Wiping some of the slick from her pussy onto my thumb, I pressed around her sphincter. The moistness was working. Her anus slowly relaxed as I twisted the tip of the anal plug inside her, and she let out a yelp.

"So tight," I said. "Your tight little hole is resisting me, Keera. I'm sure you didn't fight off Silus or Darius's dick when it was deep inside it. And this plug is much smaller."

"You're a jerk," she said as more slick dripped from her pussy. She was clearly horny but was purposely trying to resist me. She was lowkey rebellious, and I was going to have to fuck that behavior out of her when she went into heat.

I quickly shoved the rest of the anal plug inside her tight hole. Her bottom squirmed at the new foreign object inside of her. I patted her bottom and pushed the plug in deeper, making sure it stayed.

"This plug will stay inside you for the rest of the night," I said. "Shawn, release her."

She lay there with her knees up, the plug tucked deep inside her. The ruby-red jewels peeked out between her pale cheeks. Still sitting between her legs, I spread her knees apart and gazed at her dripping pussy. Her butt looked splendid, all plugged up.

Next, I grabbed the vibrator. It was a long green tube-like device with a bumpy surface, like a green monster's penis.

Turning it on, I pressed it directly on her clit, and she yelped at the impact.

The vibrator twisted and turned like a caterpillar as I slowly pushed it inside her pussy. Her eyes rolled back, and her hands gripped the sheets. My tongue shot out as I licked her clit furiously. Lapping up her pussy juices as it dripped from her pussy. Her pussy began to clench, and I quickly removed the vibrator.

"No!" she screamed, trying to kick me now. I smiled wickedly. "Keep going. Please, Jatix, you can't do this."

"I can, and I will," I growled against her pussy. My hot breath deliberately teased her swollen clit. "You will now sleep with all of us around you. Silus and Darius, you can join us now so we can rub our bodies against hers."

"That's not fair," said Silus. "Why aren't we allowed to get some pussy?"

"If she goes into heat, I'll forgive you, and then you can touch her there," I said sternly.

"What if it doesn't happen?" said Darius as he stripped off his clothes.

"It will," I said confidently. "No omega is immune to the alpha touch. She *will* want to be rutted, and she *will* go into heat."

Chapter 20

Keera

I stretched, yawning as I looked around at all the men around me.

The early morning sunshine peeked through the closed curtains. The room was humid, with everyone's scents on me and all over the blankets. Darius slept peacefully beside me, his hand resting on my left breast. I no longer had handcuffs on since Jatix had finally said the session was done at two a.m.

All night every hour, Jatix or Shawn was licking my pussy.

I had to swear that I wouldn't touch myself for him to remove my handcuffs. It was the hardest thing in my life, but by then, I was tired. I didn't know how long Jatix played with my pussy while I slept, but now I felt sore, especially in my ass, where the anal plug stayed locked inside me.

My body felt hot and sore as I slowly got out of bed, trying not to wake up the sleeping men. Silus lay sprawled on the end of the bed on his belly, his long arms hanging off the side. Shawn snored on the floor, and I had no idea how the hell he got there.

Jatix's eyes looked restless under his eyelids. Maybe he was still anxious about this entire thing about bringing me to heat. Hopefully, he wasn't having nightmares that I would never bear a child for him.

I needed to pee. I walked into the bathroom, and I felt the anal plug heavy in my bottom as I peed. I was scared to remove it in case Jatix decided I needed another night of teasing. The plug inside me turned me on as I brushed my teeth. It was jiggling in my anus with every move I made.

As I washed my face, I noticed my face felt a little hot. It must have been the effect of sleeping with three alphas and a delta. Cuddling all night with them would do that. When I returned to the room, I went into my nest in the corner, not wanting to disturb any of them. We all had a long night. It was all too much for me, and the exhaustion that took over me was nothing I'd ever felt before.

I laid in my nest, closing my eyes and listening to the birds sing. The sounds of the ocean shore combined were the most beautiful thing about Howl's Edge. I hoped one day omegas wouldn't have to be put up in auctions or seen as second-class citizens. I was lucky this pack had chosen me.

Sitting in my nest was so peaceful and relaxing with the perfect view from the window.

A spasm suddenly hit my middle, and I clenched my teeth in pain. *What the hell?* Maybe it was just the food we ate last night. I couldn't be in heat already. It was impossible. The pain passed, and I relaxed again, pulling the blankets around me.

It had to be a coincidence. When the pain hit me again, my pussy clenched, and I curled into a ball. It was like a tightening around my middle, in my womb, threatening to burst.

"Oh no," I gasped, and I saw Jatix rushing towards me. He pulled the curtain back, his hair a wild mess around his shoulders, and completely naked.

"What is it?" he asked, placing his hands on both sides of my face.

"I think I'm in heat," I said, my eyebrows furrowing in pain as another wave came down.

I felt a gush of slick expelling from between my legs.

"She's in heat!" shouted Jatix, and I heard the men exclaiming, running, and making their way to me. Jatix's cock immediately turned rock hard, responding to my heat. As I lay curled up, Jatix gently removed my blankets. "Lay on your back and spread your legs, sweetheart. I need to see."

It hurt.

Everything hurt when I turned on my back. I wasn't wearing anything, so I didn't need to mess with taking off my clothes. My pussy was clenching with need, and it felt like fire in my womb. Going into heat for the first time was exciting, but I was terrified too. *What if the pack suddenly abandoned me?* I didn't have any heat suppressants here, and I would die alone.

I felt suddenly dependent on Jatix and his pack. I needed their knots inside of me.

Jatix spread my knees apart and inserted his pointer finger into my vagina. He removed his finger, and a long stream of slick followed it. Sticky and clear.

"Sorry," I said, embarrassed as he sniffed it.

"You're in heat," he said, his face breaking into the first smile in days.

I smiled back despite the pain wracking through my body. I felt proud of myself. My father hadn't ruined me completely. I had a pack who cared about me, and I had gone into heat. It was like a weight had dropped from my shoulders. I immediately envisioned babies running around me.

"You did it," I said. "Thank you, Jatix."

"You were strong the entire night. Now it's time to relieve you and make you feel good," he said. "Are you ready for that, my sweet? My love?"

Tears came to my eyes, and I nodded.

"Do you love me?" I asked.

"I do, and I always have," said Jatix. "I'm going to stick my cock deep inside you now."

"Can I touch her pussy now?" demanded Silus.

"Yes," Jatix replied.

Darius and Shawn kissed my breasts and navel excitedly as Silus rubbed my clit. My center throbbed with the need for their knot. Fire burned in my belly, contracting and releasing as I guided Jatix's cock inside me for the first time.

"Your pussy is amazing," whispered Jatix as he plunged into me. I spread my legs wide as he pushed inside my wet needy pussy. He began thrusting slowly, getting me acclimated to his penis. I clenched my legs around his waist, desperate for him to knot inside me.

To give me his sperm.

Jatix

Keera's pussy was warm and tight around my cock.

The urge to fuck her until she couldn't think overcame me. It was my rut overtaking my thoughts and actions. Causing feral thoughts in my head. When her soft pussy hit my cock, I thrust slowly at first, trying to fight the rut.

I didn't want to scare her. But it was in vain because I couldn't fight the rut from taking over. My balls tightened as I thrust wildly into her, her legs unable to hold my waist still. When an alpha was in rut, it was hard to see anything clearly except for the need to go inside an omega. My omega lay there, her eyes wide and her pink tongue sticking out between her luscious lips. I kissed her on the mouth as I thrust deep into her, and she gasped against my mouth. I pressed my tongue into her pretty little mouth while fucking her hard. Her tongue surrendered under mine as I tasted her.

Silus rubbed her clit as I pounded into her pussy. When her pussy clenched with her orgasm, she screamed, arching her back. Her tits stood straight up, nipples hard. Darius greedily sucked on one as Shawn sucked on her other nipple.

"Jatix," she screamed as her body shook and trembled underneath me. Her pussy squeezing my cock was too much. I came hard as I pressed as deep as I could into her pussy. My cock ballooned inside of her, my semen exploding into her womb. Putting my baby in her.

A look of relief came over her face, and she kissed me hard on the mouth. I gently removed her anal plug, which popped right out.

"Do you feel better?" I asked, loving her kisses.

"I do," she said.

My lips roamed over her neck.

"You know I love you, right?" I said.

"Oh, I thought it was because you were going to fuck me," she said, laughing teasingly.

"This will show you how serious I am," I said, piercing the skin on her neck with my teeth, and she cried out panting. Her pussy clenched my cock tighter inside of her while I marked her with the bite.

"I believe you now," she gasped after being marked. She was mine. All other alphas outside this pack would know clearly that she was taken.

"The relief from your heat won't last very long," I said, laying on top of her but not putting all my weight on her as we waited for my cock to finish unloading my sperm. Silus was licking his fingers after being able to touch her clit. He was finally doing something useful. He had waited long enough. "You're up next, Silus."

Silus

Finally. Our omega was in heat, and this was the day I was waiting for. Maybe if we hadn't had sex with her in the guest house, she would've gone into heat earlier. But I wasn't going to regret a second of it. If I could do it all over again, I would. She held her stomach in pain, looking up at me.

She was waiting for me to enter her.

"Please, Silus," she said, and my heart jumped. Keera looked tantalizing underneath me, her legs open and her pussy glistening. She licked her lips, and I knew then she was looking forward to having sex with me. My dick was stone, and I needed to rut her immediately.

Leaning down to her ear, I whispered, "I'm going to take care of you now, baby."

"Yes," she moaned as my fingers caressed her pussy. She was immensely wet, her slick mixed with Jatix's semen dripping out of her. I couldn't wait to stick my dick inside her slit. I stuck my finger into her pussy and kissed her on the mouth.

Replacing my finger with my cock, I thrust into her. I held her legs up as I jackhammered into her pussy.

Giving it to her.

She seemed to like it as she screamed my name over and over.

"Fuck yes!" I roared as I slammed my rock-hard cock into her quivering soft pussy.

"Ohh," she mewled as I continued my assault on her pussy. Her slick shot out, thoroughly coating my cock.

"Shawn, rub her clit," I ordered my twin brother. He immediately got to work, and she moaned. I wanted to fucking show her that she was with the right pack. That we were the ones to take care of her during her heats.

Keera

Silus was intense, and he was sexy as fuck. I never wanted him to stop as he pounded into me. My breathing quickened with each powerful thrust of his. He held my legs up over my head, causing my pussy to tighten even more around his invincible cock. Shawn's fingers strumming over my clit nearly pushed me over the edge.

But I refused to orgasm too early. Not yet.

"Cum for me, baby," Silus growled in my ear. He knew I was holding back when he ordered Shawn to rub me. I shut my eyes when my orgasm rocked through my body. He bit me just below Jatix's mark. "Look at me, baby."

I opened my eyes, locking gazes with him. His eyes were dark with lust, and I saw the possessive look and protectiveness as he fucked me.

I cried out as my pussy released more slick, my body shaking- his mark causing lightning bolts to go through my body. Then he came next, his roar vibrating through my body. His satisfaction made it known to my omega body. His knot sealed tight inside my womb, his hot liquid spurting deep inside me.

He laid on top of me, kissing me on the lips.

"That was crazy," I said.

"I'm crazy for you, Keera," he whispered.

After his knot went down, I needed a little break despite my womb already clenching with need again.

"I need to take a shower," I groaned from the pain as I tried to stand. Silus was spent, lying on his back after knotting me. Darius gripped my arm, helping me walk to the bathroom. He made me nervous but in a good way. He was always surprising me.

"Go ahead," he said, and I stepped into the tub.

"Okay," I said, and he pulled the shower curtain open, stepping in behind me. I felt his body heat emanating from his muscular body, entrapping me in the bathtub.

"Let me get that for you," he said, taking the soapy loofah from my hand. Darius brought his hand to my front, rubbing the loofah around my chest. I felt his stiff cock press against my lower back as he washed me. He lowered the loofah, washing me between my legs.

The soft fabric rubbing me back and forth caused my pussy to clench tight. Soon his finger replaced the loofah, pressing inside my fevered pussy lips.

"That feels so good," I moaned.

"Turn around," he ordered.

I turned to face him, my hair dripping all over him from the water pouring over us. He lifted my leg onto the soap holder in the bathtub, separating my legs apart for easy access. He then gripped my ass towards him as he impaled my pussy on his cock. His hairy tree trunk legs planted between my soft thighs.

I held onto his muscular arms as I bounced on his cock with every thrust. The thick steam of the shower made it hard to see his face. We were both breathing hard, and my core clenched as I strained for release. I fingered my clit, which was covered in slick despite the water as he thrust into me.

"Ahh," I cried out, and my womb spasmed uncontrollably, milking his cock. He continued to thrust longer than all of the other guys and finally exploded inside me. He leaned down, licking my right shoulder. And then, before I knew it, his teeth punctured me, marking me as his.

"I'm your delta now," he said. "From this day forward, you have my heart, and I will protect you from anything and anyone who hurts you. I love you."

I was touched as my heart warmed to his words. He was the quiet one, but I sensed the deep loyalty he had when he committed to someone.

"I love you too," I said. "And I'm your omega. Forever."

We kissed in the shower for who knows how long until Shawn rapped on the door announcing that it was breakfast time.

Shawn

"Time to eat," I announced, handing our omega a plate of pancakes as she sat on the bed in her fluffy pink bathrobe. The house had an atmosphere of excitement today ever since she went into heat. She looked so cute as she looked at the plate I prepared for her.

"I need to eat fast before I'm in pain again," she said, eagerly grabbing the plate. As she grabbed it, I quickly squeezed whip cream and threw a strawberry on the pancakes. "Mhmm."

It gave me immense satisfaction seeing her eating my cooking. My dick hardened as I watched her lick her lips, swallowing down bite after bite. The whipped cream was smeared all over her chin, so I swiped it with my finger, licking it off. The sweetness of it dissolved on my tongue.

Oh, I wanted more.

"Why don't you lean back against the headboard and enjoy your food?" I said. "Let me feast between your legs in the meantime."

"Oh, okay," she said in surprise as she leaned back, lifting her plate up. Pulling open her bathrobe, I laid on my belly, peering at her small pink pussy tucked away in there. I grabbed the whipped cream and squirted it over her mound.

She gasped.

"What's wrong?" I asked innocently.

"It's cold," she said. "But it feels good."

"Yes. Your pussy is in heat," I said, slowly lapping the whipped cream before it hit the bed. The whipped cream mixed with her musky orange scent drove me crazy. I noticed she had shaved today as I licked her bald pussy clean. I needed her to be done eating already so I could open her up wider. The rest of the men were downstairs eating breakfast while I cared for her.

I wanted to give her relief by knotting her.

When she finished, I grabbed the plate from her and set it on the dresser next to the bed.

"Wait, my fork," she giggled, and I grabbed her fork from her hand, throwing it impatiently on the plate. I knelt in front of her and brought her face to mine. I kissed her on the mouth, tasting strawberry and whip cream. *Delicious.*

"I want to pour whip cream on you. Lay down," I ordered. My heart rate was going up as I entered rut mode. My hormones had to match hers, and I felt an overwhelming need to fuck until nightfall.

I ripped her bathrobe open as she complied.

She was looking at me with interest in her eyes. Her perky breasts jut out as I squirted whip cream over each nipple. Then I sprayed whip cream down her belly and all over her mound. I dropped the can, and I promptly got to work.

"Are you cleaning me up now?" she asked seductively, arching her hips up as I licked her nipples one at a time.

"Yes, honey," I said, licking down her stomach. Her skin was so soft. So feminine. "I have to clean your pussy now. You've been a naughty dirty girl."

"I have," she breathed. I moved down to her thighs, licking and kissing my way around her pussy. Teasing her. "You teased me enough last night, Shawn. Please don't do that again."

"I'll make up for it," I said, slowly licking her mound as I looked her in the eyes. She bit her lower lip as she gazed back at me. Her eyes lowered in desire as I licked the outside of her pussy, cleaning off the rest of the sweet whip cream. "Should I clean the inside of your pussy with my tongue?"

"Yes, and it needs something thick inside. Do you have something to put inside it?"

"I could use my cock to knot inside you."

I opened her pussy with my fingers, sticking my tongue inside her little pink hole. The warmth of her pussy closed in around my tongue. I retracted my tongue and surrounded her with my body as I thrust my dick inside her soft, waiting pussy.

"Oh, Shawn," she moaned. I loved when she called out my name.

My dick grew harder as I thrust into her. Over and over. Her breasts bounced up and down. The sight was glorious to me. So pink, so big and juicy. I grabbed her breasts while pounding into her, massaging her nipples with my thumbs. She moaned, tightening her legs around me, scratching my back as I pistoned into her tight little pussy.

I roared as jets of cum shot from my penis. And as my cock began swelling, she screamed her release, joining my roar. We were panting, holding each other in bed as our hearts beat as one against each other. We lay intertwined on the bed, my knot inside her pumping out semen.

"That was fucking amazing," I said. The relief I felt after not having sex for so long was something I couldn't explain. And it was different with an omega who cared about me. Someone who was going to stick around for a long time.

She nodded, yawning against my chest like a cat as we lay beside each other.

"Do you like me?" she asked.

"I fucking love you," I said.

"Do you want to mark me as yours?"

Fuck. From the excitement of having sex, I completely forgot about that.

"Yes, yes I do," I said quickly. "Will you have me as yours? I'm sorry I was caught up in the sex, that's all. It's not like I don't like you or anything. Because I swear, I do. I care deeply about you…"

She quietly put a finger to my lips, shushing me.

"It's okay, I understand," she said, smiling widely. "I was only teasing."

"Where do you want to be marked?"

"What's your favorite part of my body?" she countered.

Her breasts.

I lifted her full breast with my hand and licked her just underneath it. I nipped her right in that spot, and she winced. Her pussy contracted tight around my cock when I did that, and it was the ultimate pleasure of mating an omega.

Two Weeks Later
Keera

It wasn't long before we found out I was pregnant. And to my surprise, Jatix was first to find out before any one of us. As I lay in bed weeks after my heat, one lazy morning, Jatix rubbed his hand over my belly as I cuddled beside him. We were alone in bed during one of those rare mornings.

"What are you doing?" I said.

"Comforting our baby," he replied calmly.

"Baby? What do you mean?"

I hadn't felt any typical signs that I usually told omega mothers to watch for. I felt perfectly fine. Jatix must be really wishing he was a father and that my heat wasn't a waste. So I didn't pay him much mind as I listened to the ocean sing.

"You're pregnant," he said in all seriousness. "I can sense it."

"No, I'm not," I said, shaking my head at his ridiculousness. He was batshit crazy. I was the doctor. I hadn't felt a single thing.

After taking the pregnancy test, I stood shocked next to the bathroom door as I held the test in my hand. There was a giant blue plus sign on it. Tears streamed down my face in joy. I couldn't say anything as Jatix hugged me tight against his plush black robes.

"You're going to be a mother," Jatix whispered in my ear.

"I can't believe it," I hiccuped. He wiped my tears with his finger, gently kissing me on the lips.

"You'll make a damn good mother," he said. "Nothing how like my mother was."

"I hope so," I said, tenderly running my hand down his cheek. "I won't be anything like her. I can promise that."

"I know that, sweetheart."

Chapter 21

Nine Months Later

Keera

It was finally the day of the baby shower, and I was glowing. Jatix and Shawn helped put together a baby shower because it was one of the things I wanted if I was ever pregnant. Even though I barely had any friends, all of Jatix's friends were invited.

I had invited Jade and any friends she wanted to bring with her. I wore a light blue maternity dress with a headdress made of white flowers. It was simple but cute.

"That's too many snacks," said Silus, staring at the huge array of brownies and snacks I was organizing on the kitchen island.

"Doesn't Jatix have like fifty friends?" I said. "We need to be pre-pared."

I maneuvered around the table carefully, with my huge belly jutting out. The men had been pampering me for a full nine months, taking care of me nonstop, and they always got anxious if I seemed like I was doing too much work. It was sweet but also a little too much for me. I wanted a bit more freedom.

"The house is sparkling clean now," said Shawn, running around with a feather duster. He was the biggest help when it came to the party today. Silus tried to help, but instead, he managed to find time to sit down. Jatix was out buying last-minute groceries, and Darius was adjusting the furniture under Shawn's careful watch.

The doorbell rang, and my heart jumped in excitement. Our first guests had arrived.

"I'll get it," said Silus.

He opened the door, and Jade walked in, followed by three of her friends. I only recognized one of her friends. Jade wore casual jeans with a blue blazer matched with blue earrings.

"Ahh, Keera!" she screamed, setting down her gift bag and giving me a big hug, enveloping me in her raspberry scent. "Keera, these are my friends Sylvia, Gretchen, and Tiana."

"Tiana, oh my goodness," I said, turning to her. She looked flawless, wearing a pink sundress and sunglasses on her head. She was one of my patients, and I had attended her birth celebration months ago. The whole island celebrated with the Frostcrown Pack. Her alphas were well-known on the island, and I wasn't sure if I wanted the same type of celebration or something low-key.

"Dr. Keera!" Tiana exclaimed, hugging me back.

"Where's the rest of your pack?" I asked.

"They decided it was best not to show up. Considering their history," Tiana said.

"How're the twins?"

"They grow so fast! They're already running around and knocking everything down. Little Adam is a wreck," she laughed. I smiled, remembering how his eyes shined with mischief at the birth celebration. "Alana is just a darling."

I touched my belly, excited to finally have one of my own.

"Is Jatix treating you okay?" asked Tiana. "I'm sorry if I'm being rude or anything."

"No, you're good! Jatix takes care of me so well," I smiled. I understood her hesitation one hundred percent. Jatix wasn't the typical normal alpha. He had told me their history with Tiana, so I understood why she felt that way. Soon, more and more guests trickled in as I introduced myself to the other girls. Silus had turned on the music, and Jatix arrived with juice and drinks for everyone.

I stuck with water or lemonade the entire time. I was starting to feel a bit of cramping in my abdomen as I sat on the sectional in the living room, talking with Jade.

"I'm glad you're doing well," said Jade. "I was so scared for you when...that night after the ball."

I bit my lip, remembering all too well what she saw with my father.

"The nightmare ended after that night," I said. "I'm actually glad we went to the ball. I may still be stuck in my dad's house. Who knows?"

"It's a huge relief he put you up for auction. I know how bad that sounds," said Jade. "Forget I said anything at all. Fuck my life."

"How's work, though? Did they replace me yet?"

"They couldn't find a doctor fast enough. You should apply again," she said, sipping her drink.

"I'll think about it," I said. "Oh, by the way, I owe you for the dress you bought me."

I noticed that everyone crowded around the TV. I stopped and stared at what was happening, making my way to the TV. They made room for me upon noticing me, so I didn't need to jostle my belly through people.

"*We are sorry to inform you that King Saku, ruler of the Royal Pack and Howl's Edge, has passed away,*" the newscaster said.

Oh no. I hadn't known the Royal Pack too well, but I suddenly felt sorry for Princess Lyra losing one of her fathers. The guests looked shocked, some of them with their hands over their mouths.

I was about to run upstairs for the dress money when I spotted a guest with a head of stringy red hair.

My blood ran cold. My mother's killer was here. This was no imagination. Heart pounding, I couldn't move from my spot as I saw him casually talking and mingling with the crowd. The music was loud over my ears, so I couldn't hear what he was saying.

"You don't have to pay me back for that," said Jade, waving her hand dismissively when I walked to her.

"No, I want to," I said, trying to keep calm. "I'll be right back. You have fun with everyone and make yourself comfortable."

I quickly waddled to the kitchen, where Silus was passing out snacks to everyone. I saw Shawn in the kitchen, scrambling to find more snacks.

"Keera, what do we do? We're completely out," he said. "Should I just have Jatix buy more?"

"Yes. Shawn, who's that guy?" I said, pointing him out in the living

150

room.

"Oh, Grogan? He's Jatix's friend," said Shawn, barely glancing at him.

"The redhead?"

"Yep," he said.

I looked up again and saw Grogan approaching the kitchen, his eyes on me. My pulse raced as I turned away from him. He knew I was here.

"Listen, I'm going upstairs to grab some cash for Jade," I said. Shawn nodded, sticking his head back into the fridge.

Breathing hard, I climbed up the stairs. My palms were clammy, and sweat beaded down my back. I closed the bedroom door behind me and went into the walk-in closet for the cash. *Should I tell my pack?* They would think I came with all sorts of problems and baggage. First, my dad, and now this stalker.

Maybe I *should* warn Jatix. I walked over to my phone lying on the nightstand and called Jatix.

It rang and rang. There was no way he could hear his phone over the music.

I was too freaked out to go back downstairs. Maybe I would hang out here until the party was over.

As I sat on the bed, contemplating what to do, I heard a knock on the door. Oh my god, I forgot to lock the fucking door. Grabbing my phone, I ran into the closet and closed the door. There wasn't a lock, but I leaned against the door with my body. I heard the bedroom door opening, and I covered my mouth with my hand, trying not to make a sound.

Heavy footsteps came in.

None of my men wore shoes when coming into this room. It was

151

definitely Grogan.

"I've been looking for you," said a soft silky voice. I shut my eyes tight, nearly about to cry. I recognized that voice anywhere. I had nightmares and dreams about him. The redheaded monster who killed my mother.

Please, go away. Please go away, I begged in my head. Hands shaking, I felt my phone vibrate in my hand.

Jatix was calling me back.

"I know where you are," said Grogan in a sing-song voice when he heard the phone. Before I could answer, he burst into the closet, knocking the phone out of my hands. I screamed, but he covered my mouth with his hand quickly. It was all a blur as he lifted me and threw me on the bed. "Your dad said I might find you with the Lustfur Pack."

"My dad sent you?" I gasped, scooting away from him. But it was useless. He pounced on me, moving his hands up my legs.

"He was pissed you sent your little pack after him," he sneered. Up close, he looked horrible, with scars littering his face and one eye glazed over. *Was he blind in one eye?* His hair flew crazily around his face as he sat on top of my thighs.

"Please get off me," I said. "I'm pregnant."

"Your dad wanted you gone when you were sixteen. Did you know that?"

What? Did my dad send him to me the day my mom died? Grogan had to be lying.

"He only started hating me after you killed my mother," I said.

"That's not true," said Grogan. "He hated you ever since you were born. He was scared he would cheat on his wife with you. It was a mistake that your mother died. We made a deal that I would only take

152

you. He owes me a shit ton of money too, and you're the payment. Now I'll take my pleasure."

"Please stop," I begged as he kissed my breasts over my dress. I took a deep breath to scream, but he covered my mouth again with his rough palm.

"Scream, and I'll slit your throat," he rasped.

My mind was racing with what he just revealed to me. It wasn't my fault at all that Mom died. It was all Dad's fault. From the beginning, it was *his* fault. And now I was offered to pay off his gambling debt.

I nodded quickly, and he released my mouth.

"Let me get some toys for my pleasure, too," I said. "It's right here."

"Hurry up, my cock's waiting," said Grogan, pulling down his pants and freeing his penis. I didn't dare look in that direction. "This will be your last time having sex. So enjoy it while it lasts."

I rolled over and quickly opened up the drawer on the nightstand. I wanted to get away from his leering self, but he had ahold of my lower legs. I grabbed the pocket knife I'd seen on my first day here and rolled back to face him. Grogan lifted my dress, spreading my legs.

Lifting my arm high, I screamed and stabbed at his neck as hard as I could with the little knife. My heart pounded hard as I watched him glare at me. He growled, pulling the knife out. It didn't seem to faze him, even though blood dripped all over the bed.

Fuck...I was so dead.

Jatix

153

Keera hadn't answered my call.

I wondered why she called me as I opened the garage door for more guests. My mansion was full of people, and it was a happy time for our growing pack. I made my way into the house and into the kitchen. I couldn't see Keera around the living room either.

"Jatix, we need more snacks and shit," said Shawn, running around like a headless chicken.

"Calm down," I said. "Where's Keera?"

"Upstairs, I think."

Was she okay? She said she wasn't feeling well earlier. It was probably early labor.

As I reached the top of the stairs, I heard scuffling going on in the master bedroom. My heart in my throat, I raced to the door, flinging it wide open. There was Grogan on top of my omega with a knife glinting in his hand.

"*What the fuck*?!" I roared. "Get off her!"

"Come any closer, and I'll slit her throat," said Grogan, pushing her in front of him and holding a knife over her neck.

Keera looked terrified, her eyes wide with fear.

Anger and rage filled my body. *How dare he touch my pregnant precious omega?! My mate.*

I felt my body shifting, my clothes ripping apart as I shifted into my werewolf form. Only alphas could shift on Howl's Edge. Keera screamed as Grogan pressed the knife deeper into her neck. Her fear evoked a primal response from my wolf as I roared. My muscles tensed as I prepared to rip his fucking head off.

Grogan scrambled off the bed, falling headfirst on the floor in his panic.

The redheaded asshole was trying to run away. I flew towards him, and he also began to shift into werewolf form. I didn't let him, as I fastened my teeth around his neck. I telepathically communicated with my pack, which I could only do in werewolf form.

Upstairs now! Grogan attacking Keera.

Got it - said Shawn and Silus in unison.

Darius was the first to burst into the room, wielding his gun and rushing to Keera. He blocked the bed from any access to Keera, making sure she was protected first.

Shawn and Silus came in next, in their werewolf forms, both a light brown fur color. Grogan growled and snapped at me as Silus and Shawn held him down. I bared my teeth, crushing his neck. He was already dead, but Darius took aim and shot Grogan right in the chest.

I couldn't believe I was friends with this dickwad. He was dead to me.

Chapter 22

Keera

I watched as the pack hauled away Grogan's body. I couldn't believe it, and my mind was reeling from what he had told me. *Was any of it true? Did my dad want me gone since I was sixteen?* I had to talk to my dad. I needed closure. I needed some sort of justice.

The cramps in my abdomen worsened as I stood up from the bed.

"I heard a gunshot. The guests left after hearing it," said Jade, running into the room. Her eyes widened as she watched my pack shifting back into their alpha forms, carrying away the body. "What the hell just happened?"

"He attacked me," I sighed. "I'm so glad he's dead now. He killed my mother."

"He what?!" roared Jatix, dropping Grogan's body on the floor. "You never told us this Keera. Tell us everything. From the beginning."

And that's what I did. I didn't have a choice this time. I told them everything. The first time I'd seen Grogan, and what Grogan had said about my father just now.

"I have to see my dad," I said.

"Yes, let's kill him next," said Jatix.

"No," I said. "I just need to talk to him."

"Let's go right now," said Darius with a low growl.

My pack was riled up, and there was no way I could calm them down. I was furious since this was the second attempt on my life. I had no idea if my father truly wanted me dead or if Grogan acted on his own accord.

"Jade, I'll see you again another time," I said, hugging her. "Thank you so much for coming and for the gifts."

"You're welcome, my friend," said Jade. "I'll see you when you go into labor."

I knocked on the door of my dad's house. I knew my dad was home from the TV blaring from the living. I knocked three more times urgently. The door opened, and my dad peeked out. The chain blocked the door from opening all the way. He must have installed that after he was attacked. His mustache stuck out from the little opening, his beady eyes full of internal rage.

"You're with the Lustfur Pack," he said, eying my pack behind me. "What do you want bitch?"

"Grogan came for me tonight. Did you send him?" I asked.

"He's fucking stupid. Failed again, didn't he?" he grunted. "Why can't you die?"

"Did you tell him he could have me when I was only sixteen?"

He paused, his face recalling the memory.

"Well, maybe...your mother was a beta, and you're an omega. How could I resist you? The only solution was to have you dead."

"That's all I needed to know," I said, gesturing to the beta police and delta officers hiding around the house with tape recorders. Darius nodded to his fellow delta brethren. They had heard the admission of guilt, and that was all that was needed.

"Move back!" ordered a delta officer, kicking in the door. My dad stood there in shock as the dust flew around his face. He glared at me, his eyes roaming over my swollen belly.

I laid a hand protectively over it.

"I would never put my baby in danger like you did," I said with all the vengeance in my voice. "I hate you for what you did. It was *your* fault that Mom died. All your fucking fault! I hope you rot in jail."

He looked taken aback by my accusations as they stuffed him into the cruiser.

"*You bitch*!" he growled. He had always been evil, and I was ready to see him behind bars. I sighed in relief as I watched them take him away.

"Good job," said Silus, cuddling me in the backseat of the van while Shawn drove and I sat between Silus and Jatix. I was shaking uncontrollably from what just happened. All my life, I'd been scared of him. I still couldn't believe the nightmare this day had turned out to be. I was battling a ton of emotions as Silus held me, the rumble in his chest calming me. Jatix had his hand on my thigh, stroking me softly.

"All this wasn't good for the baby," said Jatix, his hand moving to my belly. "Try to relax, sweetheart."

"How could I?" I said. "My mom died, and now my dad is behind bars. I have no one."

"You have us," said Jatix. "And you'll have your little one if you try to calm down."

I took several deep breaths as we drove away from my old house. I never wanted to see it again or step foot in it. Ever again. I would sell it and take the money without batting an eye. I felt another wave of cramps hit my belly. And this time, a gush of liquid broke through, soaking the seat underneath me.

"I think the baby's coming," I said.

"Oh my god," said Shawn.

"Stay calm, everyone," said Jatix. "Let me take a look."

Another tightening around my belly. It felt like a vise trying to push the baby out. I groaned.

"Just follow my instructions," I gasped out. "When you put a finger in there, what do you feel?"

Was this the type of pain birthing mothers felt?

I suddenly had a wave of empathy for all the mothers I doctored. At the time, I thought they were exaggerating, but shit. This was too much. *Holy hell.* I could barely breathe through the pain.

"I can feel the head," shouted Jatix, no longer calm and collected.

"I thought I was supposed to have way more time," I said. "Usually, first-time births are slow, but it's happening quickly. We need to get to the hospital."

After my last coherent sentences, I took deep breaths to get through each wave of contractions. When we reached the hospital, I hoped not to see the director there who fired me. It wouldn't be a fun birth if I had to see her snarky face.

As I was rolled into one of the rooms, I shut my eyes as another wave of horrible pain crashed over me. This was too much. I contemplated pain medicines, but I wanted to experience everything. I opened my eyes to see my old beta co-worker, Tim. *Fuck this.* I didn't want him to be the one all inside my pussy.

"Is there another doctor?" I shouted.

"Why?" asked Silus. Then to the nurses and Tim. "Get the fuck away from her. We need another doctor."

"There isn't anyone else," said Tim.

"It's fine," I said, closing my eyes in pain.

"Do you want pain meds?" Tim asked. His face was twisted in empathy for me. "It's great to see you again, by the way."

"No," I said, gritting my teeth.

"Are you sure?" he asked.

"Yes, I'm fucking sure," I snapped, holding my stomach in pain. I wanted to feel everything with my first birth.

"Damn, she's vicious," said Jatix. "I'm getting turned on watching her yell at everyone."

"Shutup Jatix," I said. This pain was real, and they would never know how it felt. Darius and Silus chuckled behind me when I snapped at Jatix.

After three hours of hard labor, I was breathing hard when I could finally hold my baby.

"Congratulations on your baby boy," said Tim.

"Thank you, Tim," I smiled as I kissed the baby's forehead, softly touching his hair with my hand. I looked up at Jatix. He had teared up with tears running down his cheeks. Shawn was taking pictures at my request, and Silus kissed my cheek, also gazing at the wonder in front of us.

"I love you," Silus whispered in my ear. I turned my head up, and we kissed on the lips.

"I love you too," I said. "I love all of you."

One by one, the men kissed me on the lips while Jatix held the baby in his arms, looking at him proudly.

"His name will be Lionel," said Jatix. "Lio for short."

"Our little Lion," I crooned, smiling. "I love it."

Epilogue

One Year Later

Keera

"Lio, get back here," I called as he wobbled to the TV on his toddler legs with apple sauce all over his mouth and his teddy bear onesie. He gave me a toothless smile as he planted his messy palm all over the screen.

"Got ya!" said Silus, lifting him in the air as Lio shrieked with giggles. "Why are you ignoring your mama? You little rascal."

I was enjoying motherhood. Even though it could be challenging at times, Lio's cuteness made up for it all.

"Silus, could you wash him up? I think he's full," I said, walking into the kitchen and throwing away the rest of the apple sauce container. Jatix was leaning against the counter, chewing on grapes.

"I have a surprise for you," said Jatix, kissing my neck.

"Oh, what is it?" I said, washing my hands in the sink.

"We're going somewhere, so get ready."

"How about Lio?"

"Shawn and Silus are home, don't worry about him," he said. "Isn't that the best part of living in packs?"

"Alright then," I said, kissing him on the cheek.

I wondered what the surprise would be as I removed my dress covered in apple sauce. Maybe he wanted to take me out somewhere special. I decided to wear something nice, just in case. After much thought, I put on a light purple dress that stopped above my knee. It was strapless and fitted at the waist. I combed my hair out and put on mascara and purple lipstick. I was a little excited to be finally going out. I didn't want to leave my baby's side ever since he was born, so this would be a much-needed getaway.

In the car, Jatix still refused to tell me where we were going.

"Are we going to a fancy restaurant?" I asked.

"You'll see," he said.

After ten minutes of driving, we stopped in front of Howl's Honor Hospital. I was so confused. *What could he possibly want from here?*

"I don't have any appointments today," I said. "Why are we here?"

Jatix parked the car and fixed his long ponytail, slicking back the stray hairs. He was wearing a professional suit. The same purple one when I had first met him.

"We're here to get your job back," he said.

"No, no, no," I said, shaking my head and looking at the building. "I couldn't. It's too embarrassing. I was at a low point in my life..."

"Yes, you can," he said, grasping both my hands in his and gazing into my eyes. "I know you've wanted this for a long time, sweetheart. You want your own money and the career that you fought to have. You've become stronger now. Go in there and tell her that you want your job back."

I took in a deep breath.

He was right. I did want this job, even though it was long hours and hard work. I wanted to be the top doctor and work my ass off.

"You should have told me we were coming here. I would have worn something professional," I said.

He looked down, realizing his mistake. "I'm sorry about that. I should have known better, but you'll still get your job back either way."

"How about Lio, though?"

"He'll be perfectly fine," said Jatix. "There will always be someone at home to watch him. Especially lazy Silus. He's lazy but makes a great alpha father."

"You all are amazing fathers," I corrected.

"Now, are you ready to go in there?"

"Oh shit," I said, clenching his hands tight. "Yes, let's do this."

As we walked into the hospital, we passed by the patients in the waiting area and headed up the stairs toward the director's office. Lucia was the last person I wanted to see, but Jatix was with me. And that gave me the strength I needed.

The large redwood door looked intimidating, but I took another deep breath. I knocked two times, dreading facing her again.

"Yes?" she called. I opened the door and steeled myself, walking into the room with purpose. "Oh, it's you."

Then she saw Jatix walking in behind me, and her eyes bugged out. She stood up and offered a chair for him.

"I came to see about getting my job back. To get reinstated," I said, getting straight to the point. If she refused, that was on her. I wouldn't care after that, but at least I would try.

She started to smirk, and I could already see the refusal behind her eyes.

"Before you say anything," said Jatix. "I would appreciate you giving my mate the respect she deserves."

"Wait, what? She's your *mate*?!" said Lucia, shocked.

"She is. The love of my life," said Jatix. "So, how about that job?"

He stared her down, and she grew flustered.

"You can start on Monday," said Lucia, sickly sweet, turning to me. "You can come in and start the paperwork then and start working effective Tuesday."

Oh, my goodness. It worked.

"That sounds good. Thank you," I said, shaking her reluctant hand. She shook Jatix's hand without hesitation.

"Will we see you at the next donor meeting?" she asked him.

"It depends," said Jatix, not guaranteeing anything. It sounded like a thinly veiled threat that he wouldn't give a penny if I was mistreated again.

As we walked out of the office, I couldn't wait to celebrate with Jatix and the rest of my men. Jatix took my hand and squeezed it as we headed to the car.

"Congratulations on your new job," said Jatix, kissing my hand.

"Thank you," I said, giddy with excitement. "If it weren't for you,

I wouldn't have had the courage."

"It was all you," said Jatix, kissing me in front of his car. I leaned against the car's hood and closed my eyes from the hot sun as he kissed me again.

"Woo!" yelled Silus when I broke the good news.

Shawn gave me a big hug, twirling me around the living room, and Darius kissed me hard on the lips.

"Good job," said Darius, making my heart race with his fiery gaze.

"Tonight, we should celebrate," said Shawn.

And we did.

Jade had come over to babysit for us, and we were all crammed in Shawn's van as we drove to *The Savory Rose*. A popular alpha-omega restaurant. I dressed a little fancier in a long glittering red dress with red jewelry.

"You look absolutely stunning," said Jatix as we walked towards the restaurant while he held my hand. Silus's hand rested on my butt as we walked. I felt the familiar giddiness that I did when I was with my pack. But this time, it was full-on excitement at having my job back.

I was going to work hard and prove myself.

"The restaurant is pretty," I said, squeezing his hand.

I gazed at the stunning upholstery of the chairs and the unique way the tables were set up. There was a special chair that looked like a throne for the omega of the group. I had never been to this restaurant before. We followed the server as he graciously led us to a table.

"That's your omega throne," said Silus, pulling out the largest, prettiest chair for me with both hands.

I smiled and sat down.

Silus sat to the right of me and Jatix to my left. Darius and Shawn sat around the table. I looked at the menu and saw a bunch of fancy pasta and steaks. Growing up, I could never afford this and was still getting used to Jatix's lavish lifestyle. The boat trips and beautiful locations he and his pack took me to were splendid.

As we ate, Silus made a toast.

"To Keera getting her job back!" We clinked our glasses, and I couldn't help but wear a huge smile throughout dinner.

"I'm so excited to start and make money," I said.

"But I provide you everything," said Jatix with a glint in his eye.

"I don't think so. Remember that necklace I wanted?" I joked.

"No, I'm kidding. We're all very happy for you, sweetheart."

Silus rubbed my thigh under the table.

"We'd like to show you how happy we are for you tonight," said Silus, his voice lowered. His grey eyes had darkened with desire, and my thigh burned from his touch.

"Ooh, I'd like to know," I said, sensing the men becoming agitated with arousal as they ate their steaks. I noticed Shawn's gaze slip to my cleavage multiple times. The alphas' scents became thicker with lust, and Jatix was rubbing my other thigh. When I snuck a peek under the table, I noticed his hard-on was apparent.

Later that night, we tiptoed into our home, and Jade met us outside Lio's bedroom door. Her hair was in a messy ponytail, and her black shirt was covered in baby food.

"I put him down to sleep," she whispered as I walked her to the front door.

"Thank you so much for watching him," I said, opening the door for her. "I owe you one."

"Don't worry, I'll keep that in mind," Jade laughed. "I'll have to find a pack first."

"And you will," I reassured her. I had no doubt she would make the perfect addition to any pack. She was the kindest friend I had and so caring. "I can't wait to work with you on Tuesday."

"I can't believe you're coming back," said Jade, hugging me.

"It'll be a nice change of pace for me."

"Well, I've got to get going. Have a good night!"

"Bye, Jade."

After she left, I closed the door and walked upstairs to join the men in stripping off our clothes for the night. But first, I wanted to check in on Lio, so I quietly went into his room and saw him peacefully lying on his tummy in his crib. I kissed the back of his head, inhaling his baby scent. Upon leaving the room, I closed the door gently behind me.

When I walked into the bedroom, I was instantly surrounded. Silus leaned into my ear and twirled my hair, making my heartbeat race.

"Little Lio's sleeping," he whispered. "We need you tonight, Keera."

Shawn went around behind me and started unzipping my dress, undressing me.

"Watch how her breasts spill from her bra," said Jatix in a hoarse voice, unsnapping my bra.

"So beautiful," said Darius, cupping my breasts in his hands. Squeezing them. "Like plump melons."

My clit was throbbing to be touched, and my pussy clenched with desire.

"We're going to take you on all sides," whispered Silus, biting my ear gently. "I'm going to take your ass. Jatix will take your pussy and Darius in your mouth. While that's happening, you will use your hand for Shawn's dick. Does that sound okay, baby?"

"Yes," I gasped when Darius tweaked my nipples.

I was only wearing my black lace panties by the time I was lying in bed with all four of my men. Silus pulled me over him, my back against his lean stomach. Jatix slowly pulled my panties off with his teeth. As his teeth grazed upon my inner thighs, I shivered. Coils of warmth flowed through my body, my womb aching for their knots.

"I can smell her," said Shawn when Jatix removed my underwear. Silus spread my legs apart while he lay underneath me.

"Take a good look, men," said Silus. I felt his hard cock beneath me, ready to plunge into my ass. My heart pounded in anticipation of being filled with cock. Jatix spread my legs out further, giving my pussy one good lick. I shuddered with arousal when his wide tongue swiped over my clitoris and plunged inside me.

Darius settled over my face, his thick thighs spread on both sides of my head. His dick swung eagerly in my face. I grasped his dick and lifted my head, licking the head of it. It was thick, purple, and throbbing in every inch of it.

"Fuck," muttered Darius, pushing his dick further into my mouth. My mouth was full as I tried to bob my head, licking his cock as best as I could. Silus spread my ass cheeks apart, rubbing my anus with his finger coated in saliva. I felt his finger go round and round. Stimulating me, causing warmth to flow through me.

Jatix placed two fingers into my pussy while licking my clitoris. I felt his thick tongue pressing on my clit with urgency, and my legs trembled. I gripped Shawn's cock while Darius was still in my mouth.

I tried to concentrate on rubbing Shawn's cock up and down while all my holes were touched, prodded, and filled. I clenched my legs, overwhelmed by all the touch and feelings, but Jatix held my legs apart firmly. Silus pressed the tip of his cock into my ass, and Jatix grasped my thighs.

Not allowing me to close my legs.

"Relax," said Silus, slapping my ass. I moaned as slick released through me, and pleasure flowed through my body. I loved how Jatix was so controlling in bed but not outside of it.

"Good girl," said Jatix. "I'll open her ass for you, Silus."

To my panic, Jatix spread my ass cheeks as Silus guided himself inside me. His cock was always too huge for me back there. It stung, and I gasped against Darius's large cock inside my mouth, almost choking on it.

"Suck harder," ordered Darius. I obeyed, shutting my eyes and allowing Silus to enter me fully, stretching my anus. I slurped and sucked on Darius's cock, and his knees buckled with arousal while I pulled on Shawn's dick, wrapping my fingers firmly around it and pumping it up and down.

Jatix entered me next, his thick penis slowly pushing inside my eager pussy. I moaned again, amazed at how it felt. All my holes were filled nicely, and my pussy clenched around Jatix's cock tightly, desperate for his knot. My butt was full of Silus's cock as he thrust into me, pushing my body up and down. My breasts bounced in Shawn's grasp. Every part of my body was being used for this pack's needs.

Jatix continued to pound mercilessly into my pussy, pressing his cock as deeply as possible into me. Both Silus and Jatix were moving in a fast rhythm, dominating my ass and my pussy.

Thrusting in sync.

I sucked on Darius's cock, and he let out a roar as his cum spurted in my mouth. I desperately sucked every last drop, licking his cock clean while he grasped my hair.

"I love you, Keera," said Darius, kissing me on the lips despite the semen.

"I love you too, Darius," I moaned, overwhelmed by what was going on down there.

Silus grasped my hips, thrusting deeper inside my ass. Shawn was next to orgasm, his seed spilling into my hand. He continued to suck and lick my breasts.

"You're so amazing," Shawn groaned with one of my breasts in his mouth. My nipples were hard, and tendrils of heat spiked to my pussy the more he sucked on them. Shawn rubbed my clit as the two cocks pounded into me. "Your clit is swollen."

Darius held my right leg out wider, watching Silus and Jatix ram into me. More and more slick gushed out of me, coating both of their dicks. Shawn rubbed my clit harder, and I tensed up, feeling the impending orgasm about to hit.

Then I let it take over, and my body shook as the most powerful orgasm took over. I covered my mouth, holding back my scream as I squirted against Jatix's penis, the wetness dripping down into my ass.

"*Fuck*," said Jatix, climaxing in my pussy. Claiming my pussy as his seed exploded inside me. Hot long streams of liquid gushed into my womb as he knotted inside me. His thick cock swelled deep inside me, stretching me, holding me.

Silus was next, groaning under me as his orgasm took over. Semen spilled inside me, his cock swelling, trapping it all inside me. I was trying to catch my breath as Jatix collapsed on top of me, sandwiching me between him and Silus. Both of their knots inside me were a lot. My anus and pussy stretched to their limits, the ballooned penises sitting inside me.

Silus kissed me hard on the lips, and I kissed him back.

"Your knots feel so good inside me," I said.

"It's gonna stay inside you for a while," said Silus, adjusting himself, but the knot stayed firm inside. Holding my waist, he laid me on my side, with him still deep into my ass. We laid on our sides, with Silus spooning me from behind. I felt their hard cocks pulsing inside me, refusing to release.

"How do you feel with two thick cocks inside you?" Jatix asked, still locked inside my pussy as he kissed me.

"It's my favorite part," I said, yawning like a satisfied cat. "I can't believe the baby didn't wake up."

"You were making a lot of noise. Almost had you screaming there," said Jatix, winking at me. My face burned.

"Well, I didn't," I said.

"There's nothing to be ashamed of," said Jatix, lazily playing with my breast. "Our job is to make sure you're satisfied in every way. Every part of your body and your mind should be happy."

"I am happy," I said, kissing him again. "I'm so glad you went to the Omega Auctions that day."

"It's an unfortunate place to meet, but I'm glad too," said Jatix. "We will grow our family and make more babies."

"And make more love," said Silus, kissing my earlobe and touching my arm.

As I cuddled in with my pack, I grew excited about my future with them. I was finally home.

And I knew in my heart and soul my mother couldn't have been prouder of me for finding my true love with this pack.

THE END

Continue the adventure! Read Book 3: **Princess For The Pack**

Sneak Peek

of

Princess For The Pack

Prologue

Princess Lyra

The Royal Pack was full of secrets.

The islanders of Howl's Edge had spoken of it, yet as the princess and daughter of the Royal Pack, I had been ignorant of the gossip until I witnessed them firsthand.

Perched atop the staircase, I watched my three alpha fathers, greet their new omega into throne room. At least, I was sure she was an omega. She was young with fiery red hair and oval eyes. They hugged her in turn, and I felt sick to my stomach. The rumors were true. They *had* taken in a new omega from the last Omega Ball.

This was a nightmare in the making. King Saku, the oldest of my fathers had passed away three months ago. Barely that, and they were already acting like nothing happened.

My mom was still wearing black and mourning, for goodness' sake. Saku was the only one who held the family together like glue, his wise counsel sought after. The family bond was over once he passed away. I felt it happen after the funeral. The distance between my fathers and my mother, Queen Ophelia lengthened day by day. My fathers pounced like lions on the next omega they saw without their brother's guidance. Just because my mother could not bear anymore children.

I watched, shocked and dismayed, as the omega kissed them all on the lips. Her hips swayed seductively as she walked to each of them in turn and bile rose in my throat. They were supposed to be comforting my *mother*. Not blatantly kissing this omega for all to see.

Making my way down the stairs, I decided to destroy this little party. They all looked at me when my heels clicked on the throne room floors, announcing my presence. They quickly distanced themselves from the red-haired omega upon seeing me arrive.

King Armon, the oldest of my fathers, smiled upon seeing me. He was tall and lanky with a long gray goatee. He had taken over as king after Saku passed away.

"Daughter, meet Vanessa," he said, gesturing to the new smirking omega. "We didn't expect you'd be here at this hour."

"*King Saku* died. Not mom," I hissed. Then I turned to the omega.

"My mom is still alive and here. So why don't you pack up and go back home, bitch?"

My fathers gasped at my audacity. But I didn't care.

Vanessa's eyebrows rose, but her smile was still stuck on her face. A permanent clown face with thick red lipstick.

"Lyra's still grieving, and she's only nineteen- just a kid," said Dravin, quickly covering for me and shaking his head. His bushy eyebrows all over the place. "Let's get to know each other some more in private."

"Of course," said Vanessa in a silky thin voice, following the alphas deeper into the palace.

I felt like throwing up.

Weren't my dads too old to keep up with a horny omega?

I sighed loudly, and my bodyguard walked over to me. Luke was my friend and confidante while growing up at the castle. The only person in the world besides my mother who I trusted. He was thirty-eight, tall, and had a body made of rock, wearing his official royal guard uniform of black and red. He had short straight brown hair with youthful-looking eyes.

"You should check on your mother," he said in a low voice. "Forget what they're doing here, my princess."

"You're right," I said. I had no idea if she'd seen the brand-new shiny omega yet. "Do you know where she is?"

I had to tell my mother the news. My fathers had already found a new omega to breed with.

"She's in the library."

"Okay," I said, heading off towards the library. I walked down the vast hallways, my heels echoing down the chamber. I could already hear the giggling and moans through the walls. I covered my ears as I burst into the library doors.

My mother was sitting in a large armchair that was too big for her, sobbing into her hands. The upper half of her body was wrapped in a large black shawl.

"Mom?" I said, wrapping my arms around her in a hug. "I'm sorry."

She didn't say anything as she quietly sobbed into my shoulder. Burning tears pricked my eyes. She had most likely seen everything that transpired in the throne room.

If my fathers could act like this and throw my mother to the side like garbage, how could I trust anyone? I vowed to never let myself fall for any alpha, no matter how nice he was. Because if one day, I couldn't have babies as my mother did after her miscarriage, it would be easy for an alpha to leave.

And that wasn't going to happen to me. Not if I could help it.

END EXCERPT

Download Princess for The Pack here.

Also By Layla Sparks

Howl's Edge Island: Omega For The Pack Series (Reverse Harem Series)
Book 1 (*Tiana's story*): Stolen by The Pack
Book 2 (*Keera's story*): Auctioned to the Pack
Book 3 (*Lyra's story*): Princess For The Pack
Book 4 (*Vanessa's story*): Betrayed by The Pack
Book 5 (*Jade's story*): Matched to The Pack
Book 6 (*Alana's story*): Knotted by The Pack
Book 7 (*Lacy's story*): Craved by The Pack
Book 8 (*Olivia's story*): Freed by The Pack

Captive After Moonlight Series: DARK Romance
Jenna gets a lot more than she can handle when visiting the smutty toy shop downtown. She looks for the perfect naughty toy, but little does

177

she know that a werewolf is looking for *his* toy...
Now she's kidnapped by a psycho HOT werewolf who believes Jenna should be his.

Book 1: Werewolf's Mate
Book 2: Werewolf's Captive

Thank you so much for reading!

Please leave a review letting me know your favorite parts of the story. This helps authors like me keep producing more stories for you. To get updates on my next book and to get exclusive cover reveals and first chapters, sign up for my newsletter below:

Newsletter
Tiktok: @author_laylasparks
Instagram: https://www.instagram.com/author_laylasparks/
Twitter: https://twitter.com/LaylaSparks7

Made in the USA
Coppell, TX
16 January 2024

27778657R00111